GHOST OF GIRLBAND PAST

HARRY MCCABRE 5

NIC SAINT

GHOST OF GIRLBAND PAST

Harry McCabre 5

Copyright © 2017 by Nic Saint

All rights reserved. No part of this book may be reproduced in any form by any electronic or mechanical means including photocopying, recording, or information storage and retrieval without permission in writing from the author.

This is a work of fiction. Names, characters, places, brands, media, and incidents are either the product of the author's imagination or are used fictitiously. The author acknowledges the trademarked status and trademark owners of various products referenced in this work of fiction, which have been used without permission. The publication/use of these trademarks is not authorized, associated with, or sponsored by the trademark owners.

Edited by Chereese Graves

www.nicsaint.com

Give feedback on the book at: info@nicsaint.com

facebook.com/nicsaintauthor
@nicsaintauthor

First Edition

Printed in the U.S.A

PROLOGUE

*L*ondon Borrow of Hackney, August 26, 1997

Five women stood staring down into the freshly dug hole. They gazed dispassionately upon the body of the man they'd just killed and unceremoniously dumped into the hole. Rain was lashing the earth with a dull thrumming sound, stirring up a musty scent that filled their nostrils, rivulets of muddy water flowing into the pit. They were soaking wet and streaked with mud, but they didn't care.

"Is the monster dead?" asked Janell. Her red hair was plastered to her skull and she was shivering violently. "Is it really dead?"

"It is," said Carrie, the sporty one amongst the five friends. "We've slain it."

"I can't believe it," said Janell.

"What can't you believe?" asked Amaryllis. "That it's dead or that we killed it?"

"Both."

"Better believe it," grunted Courtney. Rain was streaming

down her face, which now resembled a raccoon's, her mascara creating black streaks across her cheeks.

"And now it's time to make sure it stays dead," said Perpetua, and flicked an amulet on top of the body.

Five pairs of eyes followed the silver amulet as it described a perfect arc through the air, then landed on the monster's chest, where it would make sure it would never rear its ugly head again.

Five shovels dug into the pile of dirt next to the hole and dumped the wet earth onto the body. The fifth and final shovelful was thrown down by Amaryllis, the youngest of the bunch, and the one who'd suffered the most at the hands of the man. She hesitated before tossing the soggy soil onto their victim. They should have closed his eyes. It was way too creepy staring into those dead eyes. They were fixed on her, an accusing expression gleaming in those dead orbs. As if ready to rear up, and attack them again. Finally, with a brave whimper, she flipped the shovel blade and the muddy sod dropped down, plunking down onto the man's face.

"Well done, Amaryllis," said Courtney. "Now let's pray this is the end."

"This is the end," they all murmured softly, before digging their shovels in again.

They worked in silence, as more and more of the black earth covered the dead man, soon completely obscuring him from view. When the hole was filled up, they flattened the earth with their shovels, then rolled the plaque back into place. And as they walked away, their deed done, lightning slashed the night sky, and lit up the plaque. It read: *Cardinal Yardley Roman Catholic School Time Capsule – Not To Be Opened Before 2067.*

. . .

GHOST OF GIRLBAND PAST

London Borrow of Hackney, Present Day

There was a full moon out, which made the work that much easier. Of course, it also meant they could easily be seen from the road by anyone walking their dog.

"Come on, Doug," said Ricky. "No one in their right mind walks their dog at this time of night. They'd be completely mental!"

"They might," Ricky said, anxiously glancing up and down the street.

The two friends had come down to the front lawn of the Cardinal Yardley School, their alma mater, to do something they'd been wanting to do since they were little kids. Now, since reaching the ripe old age of twelve, no longer boys but men, they'd decided finally to screw up their courage to the sticking point and raise the capsule.

"Do you think it's heavy?" asked Doug Adams, the fair-haired one of the two. He shoved his shovel into the ground and took out a first chunk of turf and dumped it to the side.

"I don't think so," said his best friend, dark-haired Rick Curtis. "Most of these capsules are quite small." He was staring pensively and a little trepidatiously at the ancient stone walls of the school's main building. It looked medieval, with its fortified battlements, thick masonry and heavy oak entrance door. It reminded him more of a dungeon than an actual school. He shivered. "This place gives me the creeps," he confessed.

"Which is exactly why we need to dig up this capsule," said Doug, his tongue sticking out while he stuck his spade into the ground again.

They'd had some trouble removing the heavy bronze plaque and dumping it to the side, and the deeper they dug, the more Rick was having second thoughts about this endeavor. "What if they put some kind of protection in place?" he asked. "You know, like in those Indiana Jones movies?"

"Are you kidding? This isn't some ancient treasure, Ricky. Just a bunch of old crap."

"If it's just a bunch of old crap, why are we digging it up?" he asked heatedly.

"There might be some fun stuff in there," said Doug, always the more adventurous of the twosome.

"Like what?"

"Like Mrs. Rampart's knickers."

Rick grinned. He would like that. He hated Mrs. Rampart's guts. Ever since she'd punished him for accidentally aiming a soccer ball straight through the library window, she'd had it in for him. "We could fly her knickers from the school flagpole!"

"Or we could boil them down and make Mrs. Rampart Knickers Juice! We could bottle it and sell it and make a fortune!"

"Or we could stick it on the head of Cardinal Yardley himself!"

They both looked up at the statue of the old cardinal, which stood sentinel in front of the school, his eyes staring manly up at the sky, his long beard brandishing in the wind, his funny-looking hat slightly askance, as if he'd dipped into the sacramental wine again. Both boys' eyes gleamed. Yeah, this was a right great scheme: dig up Mrs. Rampart's knickers and stick them on the head of that old fruitcake Cardinal Yardley.

With renewed fervor, they dug their spades in. It was hard going, and the capsule proved to have been buried a lot deeper than they'd anticipated when they'd concocted this wild scheme, but finally Rick's spade hit something solid. His eyes went wide with excitement. "I think I've got it, Doug!"

"Go on, then. Don't stop now," Doug urged. And as they

cleared away the dirt, Rick saw something glimmering in the moonlight. It looked like… an amulet.

"Hey, look at that!" said Doug. "We found treasure after all!"

Rick reached down and picked up the amulet. He removed the caked earth and twisted the precious find in his fingers.

"I think it's silver," said Doug, his voice reduced to an awestruck squeak. "Regular silver!"

"There must be more," said Rick, and started removing the dirt with his hands.

He felt it before he saw it. There was something mushy under his hands. Something soft and squishy. And when he finally reared back, a scream stifled in his throat, Doug asked, "What is it? What's wrong, Ricky?"

He gestured at the face of the man he'd just uncovered. "It's—it's—it's a body, Doug! There's a dead body down there!"

And then they were both screaming.

When they'd finally recovered their sangfroid, Doug said, "We have to bury it again. No one can know we were here."

Rick quickly agreed. He could just imagine what his parents would say if they found out that instead of having a sleepover at Doug's place, he was digging up dead bodies in the middle of the night.

They quickly shoved the dirt they'd removed back into place, then placed the clumps of turf on top of them and rolled the plaque to cover up the damage they'd done. When they were finished, no one could see that the site had been disturbed. And as Rick threw one final glance at their handiwork, a glint caught his eye. And then he saw it: Doug was throwing the silver amulet in the air and deftly catching it again.

"Did you take the amulet?!" he cried, aghast.

"Of course I did. It's ours. We found it fair and square."

He had to agree that his friend had a point. "Well, I found it, actually."

"We both found it."

And as they walked away, dragging their shovels behind them, they agreed that they would share ownership of this new and exciting treasure. Doug would get to keep it one week, Rick the other. That was only fair.

"Who do you think that body belongs to?" asked Rick.

"Old Yardley, of course," said Doug. "Who else?"

Ricky shivered. "I hope he won't put a curse on us."

"No, he won't. We buried him again, didn't we? Trust me, Ricky. It's fine."

"Do you think we should have called the police?"

"Are you nuts? For digging up the cardinal? We'd be expelled!"

As usual, Doug was right. And as Rick palmed the amulet, his nails removing some of the dirt, he asked, "How much do you think this amulet is worth?"

"Millions," said Doug knowingly. "Maybe even billions."

His face lit up. "You think?"

"Of course. We're rich, Ricky."

"How rich?"

Dough thought about this for a moment. "At least as rich as David Beckham."

"Wow," said Rick, his eyes wide as saucers. "We're super rich, Doug!"

"Yah," said Doug with a wide grin. "Super duper rich!"

And as they walked home, he quickly forgot all about Cardinal Yardley's body. They were rich like Beckham!

CHAPTER 1

We walked the hallowed halls of the Natural History Museum, our feet sounding hollow on the stone steps as the sound reverberated in the vaulted space. As I looked around, I thought the museum resembled a cathedral more than an actual museum, and was more than a little spooky. Great place for a ghost to make a nuisance of himself.

Jarrett seemed even less comfortable traversing the hallways of this ancient place than I was. Then again, Jarrett hates both mummies and dinosaurs, so that might have had something to do with that slightly worried look on his face.

My name is Henrietta McCabre and I'm a ghost hunter—though we like to call ourselves wraith wranglers, as it sounds a little—or a lot—cooler. My associate Jarrett and myself have been doing this work for a little while now, and are usually called in when some poltergeist or other ghostly guest kicks up trouble. It was the first time we'd actually been called in to clear a museum of its ghosts, though.

"I don't like this, Harry," said Jarrett, his eyes flitting up at the gigantic skeleton of the dinosaur at the heart of the museum hall. "I don't like this at all."

"Relax, Jarrett. It's just a bunch of old bones."

"It's a dinosaur. Have you seen what they can do? I've seen *Jurassic Park*. And *Jurassic World*—you just have got to love that Chris Pratt. He's got the finest bum I've seen in the movies recently."

"Focus, Jarrett," I said. "We're here to do a job, not talk about Chris Pratt's bum."

Jarrett craned his neck to take in the enormity of the dinosaur. "That thing's huge! Where is Chris Pratt when you need him?!"

"It's a dead dinosaur," I reminded him. "It's not going to do anything. So we don't need Chris Pratt."

"You don't know that," he said. "It might come alive again. And one can always do with a bit of Chris Pratt. That man is fine."

"Will you just focus?" I asked through gritted teeth.

"Oh, all right," he grumbled, patting his hair to make sure it was still in place. Jarrett is fair-haired, slender and one of the richest men in the country. Or at least his father is. Jarrett simply sponges off the old man. As for me, I'm not rich nor come from money. I pushed at my blond bob, smoothed my pink T-shirt around my lithe form, adjusted my jeans, and walked up to the man we were here to meet.

"Hello, Mr. Goodfellow," I said. "Henrietta McCabre, but everyone calls me Harry. And this is my associate Jarrett Zephyr-Thornton."

"The Third," Jarrett added petulantly.

"So what can we do for you?"

Julian Goodfellow was younger than I'd imagined and rocking a sexy bookish look, with a pair of horn-rimmed glasses on a well-shaped nose, his handsome face creased into an engaging smile. When he gripped my hand and shook it, there was power in those fingers.

"So nice to finally meet you, Harry. Your reputation precedes you. And you, Jarrett."

"H-hi," said Jarrett, slightly taken aback. "You've got a-a firm grip, Mr. Goodfellow. Do-do you work out?"

I rolled my eyes. When Jarrett starts stuttering, it's usually because he's spotted prey. It's part of his Hugh Grant impersonation, which he figures will add to his charm.

"I do work out, yes," said the museum director after a pause. "It's important to stay in shape."

"Oh, absolutely," said Jarrett. "I work out myself, of course. Not a day goes by that I don't spend in the gym. And the sauna, of course. Nothing like a nice sauna after a hard, hard workout." He gave the other man an appraising look, but the director ignored him.

"So. Shall we?" he asked, directing an expectant look at me.

"Yes, let's," I said, after giving Jarrett a nudge.

"What?" he hissed when we both fell into step behind Julian.

"This is not the time to hit on the guy!" I hissed back.

"I'm not hitting on him! I'm just... being nice."

"Nice! You practically invited him to share a sauna!"

"I did not. I was just exchanging pleasant banter."

"Well, save it for later. We're here to do a job, not to pick up a date. Besides, what about Deshawn?"

"What about him?"

"I thought you guys were happy together?"

He gave a noncommittal shrug. "He's cheating on me."

"What?!"

"If you haven't heard, Deshawn's joined *The Great British Bake Off*."

"He's cheating on you with Paul Hollywood?!"

"Well, I don't think so, actually. But he is having a ball."

I frowned. Having a ball at a baking show didn't exactly constitute cheating. And then it hit me. "I know what this is. You're jealous!"

"I am not!" he said.

"You're jealous because Deshawn is suddenly getting all the attention and you're not."

"You're bonkers," he muttered, looking away, which was as much an admission as if he'd come right out and said it. "It's just not much fun to see my better half having so much fun without me, that's all."

I smiled. Deshawn Little had been Jarrett's 'man' for years, until they both confessed to harboring feelings for each other deeper than merely being master and servant allowed. They'd been inseparable ever since. Until now.

"As long as Deshawn doesn't take his baking skills into Paul Hollywood's personal kitchen, you're fine," I said.

He grumbled something, but we'd arrived in the Ancient Egypt room, and there was no more time for idle chitchat about Deshawn's baking adventures.

"Here we are," said Julian with a wave of his arm.

The room was relatively dark, with several mummies on display, along with sarcophaguses, gilded masks, and wrapped and unwrapped remains of people who'd long been dead. It was all very impressive, and a little disconcerting at the same time.

"Are these... real mummies?" asked Jarrett, gulping slightly.

"Yes, they are all very real," Julian confirmed.

Jarrett produced a soft whimper, and I patted his back. "They're all quite dead, Jarrett," I said. "Just like Dippy the Dinosaur."

Julian stopped in front of a mummy that had been put

upright. It was stiff as a board, and thoroughly wrapped up, except for its head, which was a mere skull.

"This is the one," Julian said. "We call him Snoopy, as he resembles a beagle."

I looked closer, and saw that the museum director was right. The mummy did resemble a beagle, with its pronounced set of choppers and its equally pronounced grin.

"He looks like he's smiling," I said.

Julian now displayed a smile himself. "He does, doesn't he? In life, he was a minor pharaoh. In death, he's the pride of our modest little collection." His smile faded. "Or at least he was, until he started behaving badly."

"What does he do, exactly?"

"Well, he seems to get a kick out of scaring the living daylights out of everyone who comes near, though his favorite thing seems to be scaring kids into a decline."

"Perhaps he was bullied and this is his chance to get back at his bullies?" Jarrett suggested.

"Whatever's going on, it's a damn nuisance. We've had to close down the entire exhibit, one of our most popular ones, I might add, and visitors have been staying away. This joke is costing us heaps of money."

"I would think a museum could exploit this as a genuine selling point," I said. "Mummies come alive? An actual Egyptian mummy haunting the Ancient Egypt wing?"

"You would think that, wouldn't you? But you would be wrong. People love ghosts in theory, not when they're actually confronted with them."

"What—what does he do, exactly?" asked Jarrett. He'd moved back a few steps from Snoopy, eyeing the mummy anxiously.

"What doesn't he do? He makes faces at people, chases them around the room, and—worst of all—he spews some kind of pea-green slime at them. It's disgusting. In fact he got me just this morning. I had to put on a fresh suit before you arrived."

I assured the museum director that all was fine, and that we had the situation well in hand. He excused himself, and then hurried away, being careful to close the door behind him when he left. And then it was just me and Jarrett. And Snoopy.

CHAPTER 2

"So how do we do this?" asked Jarrett, licking his lips nervously.

"Why don't we just call him and see what happens?" I suggested.

"Right," said Jarrett, hopping from one foot to the other. "You know, Harry? I would feel a lot more comfortable if Buckley was here."

"We can do this," I assured him. Though if I was honest, I'd have preferred our third associate to be here with us, too. Sir Geoffrey Buckley had been my employer until his untimely demise, and was now our ghostly consultant, the person with his feet firmly in the world of the wraiths. Lately he'd made himself more and more scarce, however, and I was starting to think he was tired of spending time in both worlds.

I took up position in front of the mummy, which was leering at me. It was one of those juicy mummies, with quite a bit of flesh on its bones. "Um, Snoopy?" I asked, then figured this might not be the best way to address the irate ghost of a pharaoh. I glanced at the name card that identified him as Rhamenas, the sixteenth pharaoh of the Eighteenth Dynasty of Egypt, who'd reigned from 1292 to 1292 BC.

"Very short reign," Jarrett whispered.

"Only a couple of months," I whispered back.

"Probably murdered. Which would explain the foul attitude."

"Mr. Rhamenas, sir?" I asked. "Are you there?"

No response. The dead pharaoh's eyes remained as dead as before.

"Maybe he barfed up so much this morning he needs a break?" Jarrett suggested.

"Or maybe he knows we're here to get rid of him."

"About that, Harry," Jarrett said. "Don't you think it's time we start suiting up for these assignments? I mean, look at the Ghostbusters. They've got all this cool gear. Proton blasters and whatnot, and what have we got? Nothing! I mean, it's just ridiculous."

"Ghostbusters don't exist, Jarrett," I reminded him. "It's just a movie. Proton blasters or whatever don't exist in the real world. They're props."

"It could exist. Just say the word and I'm sure I could find us some stuff."

"I don't think so," I said. "Let's just keep doing what we're doing, which is simply pointing out to these lost souls that they need to move on."

"One of these days that's not going to work anymore. We're going to come up against a spirit who doesn't want to move on. A spirit so evil diplomacy isn't going to do diddly—"

Just then, the mummy moved! Or at least his lips moved. Slowly, those leathery, blackened lips opened, and before I could duck, a stream of green gunk shot out from the mummy, and hit me straight in the face!

"Duck!" said Jarrett. Royally late, of course.

I ducked, and Jarrett, instead of following his own advice, just stood there, and was now in the line of fire, taking a big hit of slime. "Yuck!" he yelled, when he'd finally sank down to his knees. "It's in my mouth! Harry, it's in my mouth!"

"It's in my eyes," I said. "Just keep calm, Jarrett. It's just ectoplasm. We know the drill."

"That doesn't mean I have to like it!"

I got up, this time making sure I kept a safe distance from the mummy, and planted my hand on my hip. "Mr. Rhamenas, what is your problem? Huh?"

"You assume he speaks English," said Jarrett, spitting out green goo.

"I'm bored," suddenly a voice sounded. "Bored to tears. Wouldn't you be bored to tears if you just had to stand there, stiff as a board, for years and years and years?"

I looked up, and saw that the mummy's lips had moved. "You speak English?"

"Of course I do. I've been in this country for so long I speak the natives' lingo perfectly."

"So you're bored, huh?" asked Jarrett. "Then why don't you just, you know, move on or something?"

"I can't," said the mummy sadly. "Trust me, I've tried, but I just seem to be stuck here for some reason." He shrugged. "So I have a little fun at the expense of those damn tourists who stare at me all day long."

"Why do you pick on the kids so much?" I asked.

"Oh, God, don't get me started on the kids," he said. "They are the absolute worst. They like to stick needles in me when they think the guard isn't watching, or even light matches to my wrappings, or cut them with a knife hoping to find amulets hidden inside. It's maddening, I tell you."

Jarrett nodded. He wasn't too keen on kids himself, and could see where Rhamenas was coming from. "So maybe you've been separated from a loved one?" he suggested. "A girl you were keen on marrying—or a guy?"

"Nope. Too busy with affairs of the state to think about dating. Hell, I'm only twenty-one, buddy."

"Oh, you're a handsome young devil, aren't you?"

"Yep. I was a big hit with the ladies," Rhamenas confirmed with a horrible grin.

"Why did you die so young?" I asked. "It says here you only reigned a year?"

"A year?" he scoffed. "I wish! I reigned for all of five months and two weeks!"

"What happened?"

"No idea. I was going to invade the Levant again—that's what we did in the olden days when we got bored—when I suddenly got sick and died."

"Poison?" Jarrett suggested.

"Could be," the Pharaoh admitted.

"Look, whatever it was," I said, "you have got to stop harassing the visitors."

"Oh? And why would I do that? Like I said, it's the only entertainment I have."

"Hey! Why don't you listen to the lady and buzz off!" suddenly another voice piped up. It seemed to come from across the room. Another mummy was moving in its open sarcophagus, and he did not seem happy.

"You buzz off, Uncle Albinium!" Rhamenas cried.

"If I have to listen to your whining one more day I'm gonna expire!"

"For your information, you're dead already."

"Oh, and I don't know that? Who do you think made me this way?"

"You're blaming me?"

"We're all blaming you, young Rhamenas," another voice spoke. It belonged to the mummy of a female.

"Mom, I was talking to Uncle Albinium."

"Don't speak to your mother like that, Rhamenas," growled a male voice. "Show some respect."

"Oh, shut up, Dad. I wasn't talking to you, either."

Jarrett and I shared a look of concern. Looked like all the mummies in this place were suddenly coming alive. This did not look good!

"Why are you all still here?" I asked. "You've been gone for thousands of years."

"And whose fault is that?" asked Uncle Albinium. "That good-for-nothing Rhamenas killed me!"

"And me," said the Pharaoh's mother.

"Add me to the roster," grumbled his father.

"Wait, you killed your entire family?" I asked.

"Of course I did! How do you think I managed to become Pharaoh at such a young age? If I'd have waited, I'd never been Pharaoh. Don't think I didn't know you were all scheming behind my back. You were going to have another baby, weren't you?"

"None of your beeswax," said the Pharaoh's mother sharply.

"We weren't scheming," said Uncle Albinium. "We were simply concerned about your mental health, that's all."

"Oh, you were worried about *my* mental health? Maybe you should worry about yours, you old fruitcake."

"I'm not the nutcase in this family. You are!"

"No, you are! You're all nuts!"

"Sticks and stones, Rhamenas! Sticks and stones!"

"I think we better get out of here," I whispered.

"I think you're right," Jarrett whispered back.

So we snuck out of the Ancient Egypt room, leaving Rhamenas and his family to fight amongst themselves. When we encountered Julian, I told him he needed to separate the family members. Only then would he ever have a hope of removing these annoying disturbances from his museum.

"I didn't even know they were related," he said, surprised.

"Rhamenas killed his own parents and his uncle, because he felt they were trying to keep him from becoming pharaoh," I explained. "And by putting them all in the same room, you simply reignited these centuries-old resentments."

"They never were in the same room before," said the director. "We just thought it would be interesting to have them all in one collection. They were spread out across the globe before."

"Trust me," said Jarrett. "Spread them out again. It'll fix all your problems."

And as we walked away, we could still hear Rhamenas fighting with his family. "This doesn't bode well for the Wraith Wranglers, Harry," said Jarrett, a worried frown on his handsome face.

"What do you mean?"

"We've never failed a client before."

"We didn't fail Julian. He just has to split up the quarreling family and he'll be fine," I argued.

"I don't know," he said, shaking his head. "I have a very bad feeling about this." He checked his watch. "Oh, shoot. I'm going to be late."

"Late for what?"

"Deshawn is on the Graham Norton Show. They're taping it right now. Wanna come?"

And so, even though I didn't know it at the time, began the next great adventure of the Wraith Wranglers.

Jarrett's words would soon prove true.

CHAPTER 3

Sitting in the audience at the Graham Norton Show was quite the experience. We got some of the best seats in the house, right in the front row, where we had a good view of all the action. Deshawn was seated next to talk show host Graham Norton, whose eyes were sparkling with mirth as he interviewed the former butler. Next to Deshawn sat Marisol Glee, the famous singer with the golden pipes. The notoriously volatile diva did not look happy that all the attention was now going to some baking Jeeves.

"So you were an actual butler, were you? Amazing," said Graham.

"Yes, and now my former employer is my boyfriend," said Deshawn, a soft-spoken, stocky man.

"I can't believe this," said Norton, rubbing his graying beard as he gazed into the camera. "This is like *Pretty Woman*, people, only much, much better! Hollywood, you have got to turn this man's story into a movie!"

"Starring Matt Damon," said Deshawn with a slight smile.

"Oh, why not? And who's going to play your boyfriend?"

Deshawn glanced into the audience at Jarrett, and said, "Ryan Gosling, of course."

"Of course," said Graham. "Matt Damon and Ryan Gosling. I would see that movie! Wouldn't you see that movie?!"

The audience burst into loud applause.

"Yes, you would, wouldn't you?" said Graham, also applauding.

And Deshawn? He just sat there, that same small smile on his face.

"I had a butler who baked once," said Marisol now, with customary affectation. "You wouldn't believe the things he did for me. It boggled the mind." She smiled at the camera and adjusted her ultra-tight miniskirt.

"You don't say," said Graham, making an effort not to roll his eyes. "Now, Deshawn. Tell me more about *The Great British Bake Off*. I'm dying to know what you think about Paul Hollywood. Simply scrumptious, isn't he?"

"He has a very impressive presence," Deshawn agreed. "Though not as impressive as my boyfriend Jarrett Zephyr-Thornton, of course."

"Oh, you are an infatuated little birdie, aren't you?!" Graham exclaimed.

"I had a bird once," said Marisol with a stiffish smile.

"I'll bet you did," said Graham. "What is your favorite pastry, Deshawn?"

"Well, I love a good Bundt cake," Deshawn admitted.

"You can never have too much Bundt cake," Graham agreed.

"I ate a Bundt cake once," Marisol began.

"Of course you did," Graham said acerbically. "Do you see yourself winning the competition, Deshawn?"

"I'm certainly going to give it my all, Graham."

Jarrett let out a soft sigh. "Deshawn is handling himself so well, isn't he? And look how photogenic he is. The cameras simply adore him."

"I thought you didn't like all this newfound attention he's getting?"

"I don't—but I have to admit he's crushing it, darling. Simply crushing it."

And he was. At least until the next guests appeared. Which is when Jarrett lost it.

"Ladies and gentlemen," said Graham Norton. "The moment you've all been waiting for has finally arrived. Please welcome onto the stage, the one and only... Piquant Pack!"

"Omigod!" cried Jarrett, his hands flying to his face. "Omigod!"

One by one, the members of the legendary nineties girl band walked onstage, announced with thunderous voice by Graham. "Piquant Red, Piquant Blue, Piquant Blond, Piquant Pink and Piquant Black, ladies and gentlemen. Reunited for the first time in twenty years, exclusively on the Graham Norton Show!"

"Omigod, omigod, omigod," Jarrett was whispering, in total shock.

"Don't tell me. You were a fan?" I asked.

"Who wasn't?!"

"Well, since I was only three when they split, I guess I wasn't."

"I love them," he breathed, eyes goggling. "I've been waiting for this moment for-ever!"

I watched as the five women walked on stage. I vaguely remembered the band, having heard their songs on the radio over the years, though I wasn't really familiar with their work. They'd done their hair the same way they used to: Janell Nodding was rocking a flaming red mane, Carrie Dobbins a cool blue, Amaryllis Gutenberg a lustrous blond,

Courtney Coppola piquant pink and Perpetua Roman a striking black. Together they were the Piquant Pack, and judging from the roar of the audience, they were as popular now as they were then.

They all took a seat on Graham's trademark red couches, right next to Marisol Glee, who didn't look impressed, and Deshawn, whose eyes had a glazed look, and I thought I could see his lips forming 'Omigod!'

"Don't tell me. Deshawn is a fan, too?"

"Only the biggest fan in the universe! No. Wait. That's me!"

"So is it official?" asked Graham. "Is the band getting back together?"

"I don't know," said Janell pensively. "Let me have a think."

"Oh, you tease," Graham laughed.

Amaryllis leaned in and touched Graham's knee. "Would you like us to get back together, Graham, darling?"

"Would I?" gushed Graham, mugging for the camera. "Would I?!"

"I'll take that as a yes," said Courtney with a grin.

"Will you tell him, Perpetua?" asked Carrie.

Perpetua nodded stiffly. Outfitted in a form-fitting black dress, she looked more like a model than a singer. Then again, she was the one who'd married the famous soccer player. After a pregnant pause, she said, "It's a yes, Graham. The Piquant Pack is getting back together."

"Ooh-wee!" cried a visibly touched Graham. "At last!"

"We're launching our new single tonight," Carrie added, "and tomorrow we're going on tour again!"

Next to me, Jarrett looked like he was about to expire. "Take it easy," I told him. "It's just a band."

"Just a band?!" he cried. "This is the Piquant Pack! The most iconic girl band in the history of the world!"

And then, as if to prove his words, the five women spontaneously launched into an acapella version of their greatest hit *Hungry*. Their voices sounded great together, and judging from the whimpering sounds from Jarrett, it was a big hit with the audience. For the chorus, they moved to the small stage, and when the music set in, they launched into a full-blown version of the song. It was quite moving, and I actually enjoyed it.

"Hey, they're pretty good," I said.

"Of course they're good," said Jarrett. "They're the Piquant Pack."

Suddenly, the lights went out, and the sound from the speakers dropped away. The now tinny-sounding voices of the five singers continued for a while but then fizzled out.

"What's going on?" I asked.

"All part of the show," Jarrett assured me. "Just making a big splash."

But judging from the angry cries from Graham and his crew, this wasn't part of the plan at all. Then, out of the blue, suddenly flashes of light crackled overhead, as if the roof had opened up and lightning slashed the sky. And then, like a supernatural deity, a booming voice sounded. "To all you silly little sycophants, be forewarned! The Piquant Pack are not what they seem!"

"What's this?" asked Jarrett.

"All part of the show?"

"I don't think so," he said.

And then I saw it. A translucent figure descended from the ceiling. He was large and looked like he was covered in fluorescent paint. And judging from the open-mouthed expression of horror on Graham Norton's face, this was not part of the plan.

"You think you can come here and announce your comeback without me?!" the voice thundered. "Well, you've got another thing coming! I will have my vengeance! Before this is over, you'll all get what you deserve!"

At this, twin balls of lightning flashed from the ghost's hands and hit the stage. The five women cried out in anguish and dove out of the line of fire. The bolts hit the stage, one taking out the famous red seat, the other one of the cameras, the cameraman only just in time managing to dive for cover. The acrid smell of burned plastic filled the air, as did a light fog that descended upon the small studio.

And then… the phenomenon ended as abruptly as it had begun. The lights switched back on, and the ghost was gone.

"Who was that?" I asked.

Jarrett nodded knowingly. "Aldo Brookfield. The Piquant Pack's manager. Only…"

"Only what?"

He turned to me. "Aldo disappeared in 1997, right before the girls split up."

I gave him a grim-faced look. "Looks like he didn't disappear. Looks like he died."

CHAPTER 4

We were on our way to the exit when an anxious Deshawn halted us in our tracks. All around us, panicked audience members were shuffling on, ushered out by an equally rattled crew. Wails of shocked emotion rent the air, and the fact that the lights were still flickering to an eerie beat didn't help matters.

"You have to come with me," said Deshawn urgently, clawing at Jarrett's arm.

"Come with you where?" asked Jarrett, as eager as everyone to clear out.

"The Piquant Pack. They want to talk to you."

Jarrett's face lit up with an expression of awe and childish surprise. "Talk to me?"

"Well, the Wraith Wranglers, actually. They insist," he added with emphasis.

Jarrett and I exchanged a look. "So that was the ghost of Aldo Brookfield," I said.

"Of course it was. Trust me. There's no greater Piquant Pack fan than me," said Jarrett.

"What did they say, exactly?" I asked Deshawn.

"We were all escorted off the stage, Marisol, the girls and Graham and I, and into our respective dressing rooms. I could see the girls huddling together, darting curious glances at me, so obviously I went over to offer my services."

"Obviously," said Jarrett acerbically.

"They asked me if it was true that I was involved with the Wraith Wranglers, and when I said I was, they huddled together once more. When they finally came out of their huddle, they turned to me and asked me to put them in contact with Harry and Jarrett."

"Those were their exact words?" asked Jarrett. "They didn't say Jarrett and Harry, by any chance?"

"What does it matter?" I asked.

Jarrett grumbled something, and we followed Deshawn up to the stage and then behind it.

"We're backstage at Graham Norton," Jarrett whispered.

It was only a short walk to the dressing rooms. I could see a rattled Graham Norton being calmed down by an assistant, mopping up the show host's brow with a monogrammed towel.

"And now we're watching Graham Norton being mopped up by an assistant," Jarrett whispered, keeping up his running commentary.

And then we arrived at the Piquant Pack's dressing room. Upon entering, it became clear that the five women had been badly shaken by the events that had just taken place. Two of them were pacing the room nervously, while the other three sat on white leather couches, having a sandbagged look in their eyes.

"Ladies," said Deshawn with his trademark soft voice. "Meet the Wraith Wranglers. Harry and Jarrett, meet the ladies of the Piquant Pack."

"Would it hurt you to say Jarrett and Harry?" hissed

Jarrett. Then, to the five ladies, he added, "It's an honor. A pleasure. A privilege. In fact it's a dream come true."

Janell, the red one who appeared to be the leader of the pack, ignored Jarrett and gave me an anxious look. "Can you help us, Miss McCabre? We're being stalked by a ghost. An actual ghost."

"We don't know if it's him," said Carrie, who was the blue-haired one. "It could be any ghost. Or it could just be Graham Norton having a laugh at our expense." She gestured around. "For all we know Graham could come popping out of the woodwork any moment now, and yell, 'Gotcha!'"

"I don't think you believe that, Carrie," said Janell. "I don't think any of us really believe that."

"We saw Graham Norton just now," I said. "He was looking pretty shaken up."

"See?" asked Amaryllis, the blond one. "It wasn't Graham. It was..." She bit her lip, darting an anxious look at me. "Is it true that you hunt ghosts, Miss McCabre?"

"Please call me Harry," I said. "And yes, it's quite true. I hunt ghosts for a living."

"And me," said Jarrett, plastering his most genial smile on his face. "Don't forget about me. Harry would be nothing without me, isn't that right, Harry?"

"We make a great team," I admitted. "Now please tell me, what was that thing?"

The members of the Piquant Pack shared another look, and Janell nodded, then said, "That thing wasn't a thing but a person. But before we tell you more..."

"We need to show you something," said Courtney, the pink-haired one.

"But before we do, promise you won't tell anyone what we're about to tell you," said Perpetua, her black hair as stylish as ever. She eyed me anxiously.

"Of course," I said. "Whatever you tell us—"

"We'll take with us to the grave," said Jarrett, perhaps a little rashly.

Just then, a man appeared in the doorway. He was tall, broad and physically perhaps the most impressive male I'd ever seen in my life. And he was my boyfriend.

"Darian!" I cried. "What are you doing here?"

"Harry," he said with a nod in my direction. "Ladies, my name is Darian Watley. Inspector with Scotland Yard. Mr. Norton and the production company have asked me to investigate an incident that took place here this evening?"

"The police?" cried Courtney, stung to the quick. "Norton involved the police?"

"Several people called in the incident," said Darian. "Can you tell me about your involvement?"

The five members of the iconic girl band all clamped their mouths shut and folded their arms across their chests. They weren't going to divulge anything to the authorities, that much was obvious.

"Darian," I said urgently. "The Piquant Pack ladies have retained our services—the services of the Wraith Wranglers."

"Oh," he said. "I see."

"It's a matter of some delicacy," I added. "Not to mention extreme discretion."

"Right," he said, planting his hand on his hip and fixing me with those steely gray eyes of his. "So this incident involved a, um—"

"An entity," I confirmed.

"And do they know what entity is involved?"

"Yes, they do," I said. "And they were just about to tell us."

"Right. Of course." He gave me a knowing nod. "You can rely on my discretion, Harry. You know that."

I knew that, but the Piquant Pack didn't. I turned to them. "Look, Darian may be a police inspector, but he's also a friend of the Wraith Wranglers. We've worked together on many cases."

"He's her boyfriend," said Jarrett now.

The fivesome seemed surprised by this. "Your boyfriend? A Scotland Yard inspector?" asked Amaryllis.

"Cool," said Carrie, nodding appreciatively.

"You can trust him. He won't betray your secret—will you, Darian?"

"You have my word," he said seriously.

"You want us to trust a cop?" asked Courtney, eyeing Darian disdainfully.

"He's not just a cop," said Jarrett. "He's our buddy. Aren't you, Darian?"

Darian didn't seem to appreciate the moniker as much as Jarrett did, but he finally nodded. "Yes, I'm your buddy, Jarrett."

"In fact if Darian were gay, I'd be all over him," said Jarrett. "That's how much I love this man."

Deshawn cleared his throat, like a chicken announcing it was about to lay an egg.

"But I will always love you more, Deshawn," said Jarrett quickly, pulling Deshawn into a hug. "Even though you're a star now."

"Oh, hardly a star," said Deshawn deferentially. "Merely a baker eager to share his skills with the world."

"Deshawn is in *The Great British Bake Off*," said Jarrett.

There were appreciative noises from the five singers, then Janell said, "We better show you what happened." She hesitated, then added, "Are you coming too, Inspector?"

CHAPTER 5

We were gathered on the front lawn of some old school in the heart of London. The school building reminded me of a creepy old castle, and I counted my blessings I'd never gone to this particular school. Cardinal Yardley Roman Catholic School might not have been able to contain my natural tendency to rebel against figures of authority.

"What are we doing here?" asked Jarrett, hugging himself and his flannel blazer. The night had turned cold and damp, one of those sudden shifts in the weather England is well known for. A chilly wind was slashing us, whipping at my own denim jacket.

"This is it," said Janell, pointing at a bronze plaque at our feet. It announced that here lay a time capsule, not to be opened until 2067. "See the markings?"

She was pointing a flashlight at the plaque, and I saw that the grass around it had been recently disturbed. "You think someone's opened the time capsule?" I asked.

Instead of responding, Carrie and Courtney picked up the plaque and dumped it to the side. Beneath it, judging from the freshly dug earth, it was obvious what had happened. The time capsule had been opened.

"What was inside the time capsule?" I asked.

Janell gave me a strange look. "I don't know and I don't care."

"But—"

"It's not the time capsule we're concerned with," Carrie said, wiping her hands on her black trousers. "It's what we buried on top of it."

"The time capsule was here long before we tampered with the site," said Janell.

"So what did you bury?" I asked, though I already knew the answer, of course.

"We killed our manager and buried his body right here," said Janell.

Amaryllis uttered a soft cry of shock. "When you say it like that it sounds horrible!"

"Well, it was horrible," said Perpetua. "Because he was horrible."

"You... killed your manager?" asked Jarrett. "You killed Aldo Brookfield?"

"Yes, we did," said Courtney, raising her chin. "Got a problem with that?"

"No, of course not," Jarrett was quick to say. "Killing one's manager sounds like a great idea. Just the thing to do, in fact. If I had a manager I'd probably kill him, too."

"He was a horrible, horrible man," Perpetua repeated.

"Just... how horrible are we talking about here?" asked Jarrett. "I mean, Count Dracula horrible or investment banker horrible?"

"Worse than Count Dracula," said Janell. "Much, much worse."

"He pinched our bums," said Carrie.

"Touched our boobs," said Courtney.

"Felt us up under our skirts," said Perpetua.

"And he assaulted me," said Amaryllis with a small voice. She shook her head. "It was awful. He invited me into his dressing room, and before I knew what was going on, his hands were all over me—and his lips—and then he held me down and..." She shook her head.

"If we hadn't arrived..." Janell began, her face hardening.

"Why didn't you press charges?" asked Darian.

"We were under contract," said Perpetua. "Probably the worst contract in the history of show business. If we pressed charges against him, we would have been finished. Kaput. He told us more than once that he owned us. That we were his slaves."

"You could have hired a good lawyer," said Darian.

"Well, we didn't," said Courtney, giving him a nasty look. "When we came upon him and Piquant Blond, we freaked. I hit him over the head so hard he never got up."

"And then we all pitched in and finished the job," Janell said.

"It was only when we were looking down at the body that we realized what we'd done," said Carrie with a tremor in her voice. "We'd just killed a man."

"Not a man," Courtney corrected her. "A monster."

"Worse. A manager," said Jarrett, earning him a scowl from Courtney.

"We needed to decide what to do," said Janell. "We needed to get rid of the body."

"Which we did, by stuffing him into this very conveniently available hole," said Courtney, indicating the site of the time capsule at our feet.

"But before we did, we needed to make sure that Aldo's evil spirit would never come back to haunt us," said Courtney. "Which is where Perpetua came in."

All eyes turned to Piquant Black. "My grandmother was a

psychic," she explained. "I didn't even have to tell her what happened. The moment I called her, the blood of Aldo still on my hands—" She gagged slightly, then quickly recovered. "She said that in order to protect ourselves, we had to take certain precautions."

"The amulet," said Janell, nodding.

"I quickly went round to my grandmother's house," Perpetua continued her story, "while the others packed Aldo's corpse up in plastic sheeting and cleaned up. Gran said that in order to tame Aldo's evil spirit, we needed to bury him beneath a special amulet. An amulet blessed with holy water and dedicated to Saint Jude, the patron saint of the lost causes. She gave me the amulet and—"

"We buried Aldo in a place where no one would find him until 2067," Janell continued.

"And by that time we'd all be long gone," explained Perpetua. "And then we placed the amulet on top of the body, to contain his spirit."

"And you announced your split," Jarrett finished the story. "But why? You were at the height of your success."

"Frankly we were all sick and tired of the whole thing," said Courtney. "The touring and the attention and the constant pressure. We'd wanted to stop before, but Aldo wouldn't let us. He worked us hard. Wanted to squeeze every ounce of juice from us."

"Every penny, you mean," Carrie scoffed. "Fifty percent of everything went to Aldo, the rest was divided amongst the five of us."

"That doesn't sound like a fair deal," said Darian.

"It wasn't. We were so tired that after Aldo was gone, we decided enough was enough. So after we buried him, we—"

"Buried the band," said Janell.

"And decided never to go on stage again," said Perpetua.

"And yet here you are," I said. "Announcing your comeback."

"Your highly anticipated comeback," Jarrett added.

The five women shared a look. "We always stayed in touch," said Janell. "We weren't friends before, but we became friends after what we shared together."

"We missed 'us,'" said Amaryllis with a smile. The others aahed. "No, I missed you guys, I really did! I'm so glad we found each other again."

"And who are we kidding?" said Janell. "The money they offered us for this comeback is good."

"Really good," said Courtney. "Like really, really good."

"Looks like you're not the only ones who came back, though," I said, staring down at what wasn't merely the site of a time capsule but also a grave. "Aldo has also returned."

"But Gran said that wasn't possible," Perpetua insisted. "Not with the amulet."

"Someone must have dug it up," I said. "And taken it away."

"What about the body?" asked Janell. "Is that gone, too?"

Darian frowned. "If someone had found a body here, I would have known. My theory would be that it was a couple of kids digging for that time capsule. They found the body and decided to leave well enough alone, but absconded with the amulet."

"Which leaves us completely unprotected," said Janell, shaking her head.

"You guys, did you hear what Aldo said?" asked Amaryllis, a quiver in her voice. "He's going to take revenge!"

"What can he do?" asked Courtney. "Scare us to death? He's dead, Amaryllis."

"No, he's not," said Carrie. "He came back from the dead to haunt us. He almost killed us just now. If those lightning bolts had hit us, we'd be dead right now."

"So you see why we need you?" asked Janell, giving me and Jarrett a pleading look. "You have to help us stop him. Before he kills us."

I gave her a comforting smile. "Don't worry. We'll take care of this—take care of him."

"Oh, thank God," said Amaryllis, and flew into my arms. "Thank you so much!"

"You're welcome," I said, a little undone. For one thing, I had no idea how we were going to go about this. And for another, I didn't know what Darian would say. This was, after all, a murder that had taken place twenty years ago. And when I looked up and saw his pensive look, I knew we were in trouble even before we'd begun.

CHAPTER 6

"I can't, Harry," said Darian. "I can't just turn a blind eye, even though it happened over two decades ago."

"Exactly two decades ago, actually," Jarrett chimed in. "To the day, in fact."

"But you must, Darian. Otherwise it's the end of the Piquant Pack. They'll all go to jail."

We were in my cozy little apartment, having a nightcap after our strange meeting at the Cardinal Yardley School. It was just me, Darian, Jarrett and Deshawn now, Piquant Blond, Red, Blue, Pink and Black having returned to their respective dwellings, or possibly having a late-night meeting of their own.

We were ensconced in my kitchen, what was left of a chocolate orange Bundt cake on the table. It was Deshawn's signature cake for the Bake Off, and I had to admit it was pretty tasty. My Persian cat Snuggles was lying on my lap, casually licking her tail. She'd had a few crumbs, too.

"Look, I'm a Scotland Yard man. I can't simply turn a

blind eye to murder. And that's what this was: cold-blooded murder."

"But you heard the girls," I said. "The man was a monster."

"That's no reason to murder him," said Darian. "If he assaulted them, they should have filed charges, not take the law into their own hands. This is England, not the Far West. We don't kill the people we don't like. We trust the justice system to do their job."

"Actually it was Amaryllis's word against Aldo's," said Jarrett. "And who would the judge have believed? The powerful manager or some pop starlet?"

"That's not for you to decide," said Darian, "but for the judge."

"The girls didn't tell you the whole story," said Deshawn softly. "Before you arrived, they were talking amongst themselves, and I happened to overhear snatches of conversation. Amaryllis Gutenberg is a single mother. She'd gotten pregnant when she was only sixteen—one of those teenage pregnancies. Her daughter was seven at the time, and Aldo had become interested in her."

"Interested?" I asked. "What do you mean?"

Deshawn gave me a serious look. "Not in a good way, Harry."

"You mean to say the man was…"

Deshawn nodded. "He assaulted Amaryllis, that much is true, but the main reason they killed him is that he couldn't keep his hands off her daughter."

"Oh, my God," I exclaimed. "But that's horrible!"

"Now I understand why they called him a monster," Jarrett murmured.

"This is one secret they don't want to share," said Deshawn. "They don't want to involve that little girl—who's a grown woman now, and probably doesn't know how close she came to being traumatized for the rest of her life. And how she was saved by her mother and her friends."

"That does it," said Darian in a low voice. "No way am I going to arrest these women. That man got everything he deserved and more."

"So you're going to leave well enough alone?" I asked.

"I am. Besides, it's not as if I have a body. And as long as there's no body, there's nothing I can do."

I gave him a grateful look.

"There is a body," Jarrett reminded him. "It's buried on top of that time capsule."

"Jarrett," I told him warningly.

"What? It's right there. I'm sure that if you just dig him up…"

"Jarrett," Deshawn now said, "I think what Darian means is that as long as the body doesn't come forward, he doesn't feel compelled to start a murder investigation."

"But how can that body come forward? Bodies don't come forward, everybody knows that."

"And a good thing, too," said Darian, casting a keen eye at Jarrett. "For if that body ever turned up, I would have no other choice but to look for the murderers."

Jarrett blinked, and then he finally got it. "Oh! I see. So no body, no crime, right?"

"Right," Darian confirmed. "So don't you go digging up that manager, you hear?"

"I'm not digging up anything," said Jarrett with a shiver. "Leave that to the gravediggers of this world."

"But what about Aldo's ghost?" I asked. "He's bound to cause more trouble."

"What can he do?" asked Jarrett. "It's just a pesky old ghost, annoyed that he's dead. He can scare the crap out of people, but that's it."

"I don't think that's it," I said. "Just look at what he did tonight. That lightning could have killed someone. And who knows what else he'll do. No," I added, shaking my head resolutely. "We have to find a way to stop him once and for all."

"To send his soul to the hereafter, you mean," said Deshawn.

"And how do you suggest we do that?" asked Jarrett. "Having a sit-down with old Aldo, telling him to buzz off isn't going to cut it, I'm afraid."

"Somehow we're going to have to convince him to leave this realm."

"He's not going to move on willingly," Darian now also said. "He wants revenge, and he's not going to stop until he gets what he wants."

"Is Amaryllis's grammy still with us?" asked Jarrett. "Maybe she can come up with another one of those magical amulets to drop on the old guy's corpse?"

"Let's look into that," I agreed. "That amulet kept Aldo's spirit confined to his makeshift grave for the past two decades, so maybe placing another one on his body will do the trick." I picked up a piece of Bundt cake and popped it into my mouth. "Let's just hope that whoever stole that original amulet left his body buried down there."

CHAPTER 7

Constable Donnie Ricard was manning the front desk at the Bethnal Green Police Station, close to the Borough of Hackney, his feet up on his desk, perusing a copy of *The Sun* one of his colleagues of the day shift had left behind. It was three o'clock in the morning and he was just reading about the commemorative events that marked the anniversary of the death of Lady Diana twenty years ago, when he thought he heard a noise.

Thump-drag, thump-drag, thump-drag.

He glanced up at the counter, but when he saw no one had arrived to demand his attention, he quickly returned to his perusal of the article.

It was a rather gruesome reconstruction of the tragic events that marred that August day in 1997 when the beloved Princess had lost her life alongside then-lover Dodi Fayed. Donnie was too young to remember all the details of that terrible day, but shook his head nonetheless. It had all been a setup, of course, Lady Di the victim of some nefarious plot by some nefarious characters, possibly connected to the nefarious establishment.

He looked up when he heard that strange noise again.

Thump-drag, thump-drag, thump-drag.

As if a heavy form was dragging itself across the floor.

He glanced up at the counter again, but there was still nothing to see.

He threw down the paper and stretched and yawned, then reluctantly rose to his feet. These nocturnal vigils wore him out. He didn't like what they did to his bio rhythm. Even his mum had told him he should insist on doing day shifts. But what could he do? He was a grunt so to him fell the grunt work.

He ambled up to the counter to take a look at the waiting room. Usually filled to capacity during the day, fortunately the last couple of nights had been blissfully quiet. No drunken revelers or ugly, sozzled, half-naked women hurling abuse. Those were for the weekends. And that's when his eye fell on the strange figure huddled on the floor. He gasped when he caught sight of it. It was the body of a man, dressed in lumps.

"Um, sir?" he asked, leaning across the desk to get a better look at the chap. "Are you quite all right down there?"

No response.

Tentatively, he stepped from behind the counter and warily approached the stranger. "Sir?" he asked, stirring the strange form with his foot. "Can I help you, sir?"

Still no response.

He moved a little closer still, and he was reaching for the man's shoulder, when suddenly the sack of lumps reared up, turning around to face him. And that's when Donnie jerked back, a startled cry of horror on his lips. The man's face had been eaten away, and if he wasn't mistaken, there were a few worms feeding on his eyeballs, or what was left of them.

"Aaargh!" he exclaimed. "Aaaaaargh!"

"I want to report a murder," the hideous figure gargled in a very strange voice.

"A m-m-m-m-murder?" he asked, his voice skipping an octave. "Whose m-m-m-murder?"

"Mine," said the man, but then his jaw dropped off.

"Who are you?!" cried Donnie. "*What* are you?!"

The man tried to speak, but without a mandible found this quite a challenge. Then a skeletal hand reared up, took hold of the missing body part, and jammed it back into place. A gray tongue, covered with a dark greenish mold, wagged anxiously, and if Donnie wasn't mistaken, there was an actual smile on the hideous face. "My name," said the monstrous emanation, "is Aldo Brookfield. And I was murdered by the Piquant Pack."

"W-w-w-what?" stammered Donnie.

There was an audible sigh, which sounded like the wind dragging through a thousand crypts. "My name," repeated the ghoulish figure, "is Aldo Brookfield, and I was murdered twenty years ago by the Piquant Pack! So what are you going to do about it, eh, cocky?"

"I'm-I'm-I'm going to take your statement?" Donnie guessed, and then keeled over and dropped to the floor, right next to the dead manager.

"Cops," growled the half-rotten corpse. "Still a useless bunch of—" But then his head fell off and rolled across the floor until it came to a stop against a small display admonishing that 'Opportunity Makes the Thief.'

❦

Darian rubbed his stubbled chin. He didn't enjoy being dragged out of bed in the middle of the night. At least he hadn't stayed the night at Harry's, or else she would have been inconvenienced, too. Because of the nature of his work, Darian preferred to stay at his apartment during the week, and spend the weekends at Harry's, since for some reason she didn't enjoy his apartment as much as he did. She caviled at the furnishings for some reason, which were too cold and modern for her taste.

He parked his car across the street from the morgue and got out, his long raincoat flapping in the breeze. The wind had picked up even more, and rain was lashing London's deserted streets. A lone streetlamp cast its diffuse light across the wet asphalt, creating an eerie scene. A black cat streaked past a red phone booth and disappeared down an alley, mewling plaintively. Great night to be called out of bed.

He stalked towards the old brick building with the red doors, drawing up his collar against the driving rain and was glad when he reached the entrance. Traversing the corridor of the Hackney Mortuary, his feet sounding hollow on the paved floor, he cursed inwardly. Not only was he now dealing with the ghost of some long-dead manager, but apparently he had another murder case on his hands as well. Dispatch hadn't revealed the name of the dead man, but judging from her inflection, it was a doozy.

He waltzed into the coroner's examination room and saw that the elderly coroner, his bald head shiny in the light from the fluorescent lights overhead, stood stooped over a body on his slab.

"What have you got for me, Cambell?" he grumbled.

Alfred Cambell looked up, his wizened features wreathed in frowns. With his unhealthy pallor, the man looked on the verge of death himself, the only sign of life his lively gray eyes. "It's the strangest thing, Watley."

"Strange? What's so strange about a dead body?"

"Well, this dead body was talking to Constable Donnie Ricard half an hour ago, announcing he'd been murdered and wanting to file a report."

He frowned. "Guy wanted to report his own murder?"

For the first time, he looked down at the metal slab, and he uttered an involuntary cry of shock and horror. The man on the slab indeed looked dead. Very dead. In fact, he looked like he'd been dead for quite some time.

"See what I mean?" asked the coroner, scratching his bald dome.

"I do," he said, once he'd recovered sufficiently. The man's head had been severed, and was lying crookedly against his neck. The sunken eyes, the lack of nose, lips or any other solid facial tissue, the skeletal state of his hands... "This guy's been dead for years!"

"My conclusion exactly. I would say he's been in the ground for decades. He's nothing more than a skeleton, most of him consumed by worms."

"And you're telling me he walked into Bethnal Green Police Station to report his own murder?"

"That's exactly what he did."

"Are you sure Constable Donnie Ricard wasn't drunk?"

"Pretty sure. Badly shaken, of course, but otherwise completely sober. And what's more, they've got the entire thing on tape, of course."

"Right," he said, remembering how they'd installed cameras in most police station waiting rooms.

The coroner sighed. "We're dealing with a physical impossibility here, Watley. And unless this is some clever hoax, I really cannot explain what's going on with this fellow. As a man of science I'm frankly baffled."

"So he walked in—"

"Or rather, crawled in."

"Right. And announced his murder. Did he mention a name?"

"He did. You're staring at the remains of none other than Aldo Brookfield."

CHAPTER 8

My snowy white cat Snuggles stroked against my leg, meowing up a storm. I was still rubbing the sleep from my eyes, and had trouble coordinating when I took out the big, bulky bag of kibble and strew some of it into her bowl and some on the floor. Snuggles didn't mind. She first ate the pellets that had dropped to the floor, then dug into the rest. I petted her absentmindedly. The news that Aldo Brookfield had reported his own murder had come as something of a shock to me, and I was still trying to come to terms with this new revelation.

"So Darian is going to investigate?" asked Jarrett, stretched out on my couch, his hands behind his head.

"He has to. I'm afraid he has no choice in the matter."

I walked over to where Jarrett was lounging and filled up his cup with freshly brewed coffee, then applied the same procedure to my own cup. I plunked down and dipped a bagel into the cup and ate it with relish. I was starving. This whole ghost manager thing was making me very nervous, and whenever I'm nervous, I tend to eat.

"So he's going to question the girls?"

"Yes. Though he did tell me that he's not going to hound them. He knows what happened and he's not going after them."

"He's going to let them off the hook? Even though he has a body?"

He sounded surprised, which wasn't surprising. Darian was always one to go by the book, and he was pretty much throwing out the book on this investigation. "I think the story of Poppy must have touched a chord." Poppy was the daughter of Amaryllis, the one who'd been in danger of being assaulted by the sexual predator that apparently had been Aldo.

"It touched a chord with me," Jarrett intimated. "If someone came after my seven-year-old daughter I'd probably kill him, too, and have no qualms about it either."

"You don't have a seven-year-old daughter, Jarrett," I reminded him.

"Well, I could have," he said, bridling. "Deshawn and I could adopt. What's good enough for Elton and David is certainly good enough for us."

"So are you? Going to adopt?" I asked before taking a sip of coffee.

"Well, no," he admitted. "That is to say, not right now. Perhaps at a later date, once we're more settled and all that."

I smiled. "I don't see you as a father, to be honest."

"And what is that supposed to mean? I could be a father. I bet I'd make a great father."

"Since you're pretty much still a child yourself, that's going to require a total personality makeover."

"I resent that statement! I'm the most responsible, most reasonable, most…"

He struggled to say more, so I quickly interjected, "So how are we going to handle Aldo Brookfield?"

"I know what you're doing and it's not going to work.

We're going to thresh out this whole adoption thing once and for all. Dad keeps egging me on to adopt—to provide him with some genuine heirs to the throne—and even Deshawn has uttered some noises in that direction, so it's something I need to give serious thought."

"You don't want children, Jarrett," I reminded him. "Over your dead body is what you always say."

"I know that," he said, a little peevishly. "But still. The pitter-patter of little baby feet is something worth considering. I'm not getting any younger, Harry."

"You're thirty-one!"

"So. Pretty soon I'll be forty, and what child wants a geriatric dad? I simply refuse to be a septuagenarian father like Mick Jagger. I still want to be able to lift up my child without throwing my back out, and I definitely want to be able to kick a ball around without getting winded and needing a puff from the oxygen tank. So if I'm going to do this, I have to do this now."

I stared at him. "You're serious, aren't you?"

"I am," he admitted. "I've even been reading up on the subject." He took out a book called 'Parenting for Dummies.' "Don't tell Deshawn, though. I want to surprise him."

"Oh, trust me. He'll be surprised."

"Pleasantly, I hope," said Jarrett with a smile.

On the telly, a commercial announced that *The Great British Bake Off* was scheduled to premiere later that week. They showed a short clip of Deshawn baking his fabled chocolate orange Bundt cake, Paul Hollywood watching on. Paul's blue eyes sparkled when he tasted Deshawn's proud creation and nodded appreciatively. "Our very own baking Jeeves," said Paul with a smile, giving Deshawn's back an approving pat.

Jarrett's happy smile disappeared. "That Paul Hollywood," he muttered darkly. "Look at the way he's pawing

Deshawn. It wouldn't surprise me if he's got the hots for him."

"Paul Hollywood is a happily married man, Jarrett," I reminded him. "And he's straight."

"That's what he says," he grumbled. He gestured at the screen. "I mean, who wouldn't fall for Deshawn? The man's got it all! He's got the looks, the charm, the wit. Just look at those eyes. They're practically crackling with intelligence."

"Deshawn loves you, Jarrett. He would never cheat on you with Paul Hollywood."

"I would cheat on me with Paul Hollywood," Jarrett muttered. "Old blue eyes…"

I decided to try and change the topic one more time. "So what about Aldo Brookfield?"

"What about you?" he asked in return, turning his back on Paul Hollywood.

"What about me what?" I asked with a frown.

"When are you and Darian going to start work on a flock of little Harrys and little Darians?"

"How about never?"

"You're answering a question with a question, Harry."

"So? We've only just met. Nobody's thinking about children, Jarrett. Least of all Darian."

Which was true. We'd been going steady now for a couple of weeks, and even though we'd had our ups and downs, like any couple, Darian had given no indication he was ready to take whatever this was between us to the next level. Then again, this wasn't Darian's first ride on the carousel. He'd been married before, and rumor had it his wife had left him and had broken his heart in the process. He never talked about it, and I respected that. I was starting to wonder about what kind of future we had, though.

"I think you should be the one to pop the question," said Jarrett, eyeing me keenly.

"Pop the question? What question?"

"*The* question, of course! Go down on one knee and ask for his hand in marriage!"

"I'm not going to do that," I said immediately. Not that I was old-fashioned or anything, but I still felt it was the guy that had to go down on one knee and do the honors.

"Oh, you old fogey, you," Jarrett chuckled.

"I'm not an old fogey! I just feel that Darian should propose."

Jarrett leaned forward anxiously. "Do you want him to propose?"

I hesitated. "I don't know."

"Oh, you poor darling. You're all confused, aren't you? Lay it all out for Uncle Jarrett."

"It's just that…" I held up my hand. "I don't know where this is going."

"I know, darling. I know," he said commiseratingly.

"Darian has been married before, and perhaps that's turned him off the entire institution permanently. I guess, because we never talk about it."

"Well, perhaps you should. Perhaps you should ask him straight out."

"I'm not going to do that, Jarrett. It's not the kind of relationship we have."

"Then you're in big trouble, darling. Because that's exactly the kind of conversation you should be having." Then he brightened. "You know what? Why don't I ask him?"

"No," I said, shaking my head in alarm. "Jarrett, don't you dare."

"You want to know what's going on with Darian, and I want to know what's going on with Darian. You're too afraid to ask? Well, I'm not." He patted my knee. "I'll fix this."

"No, don't fix this, Jarrett. Don't fix anything!"

"I will fix this. I will get him to reveal the truth. We'll have one of those man-to-man talks. I'm great at man-to-man talks. In fact you might say it's my specialty," he concluded with a smirk.

"If you try to have a man-to-man talk with Darian he'll beat you," I warned.

"He won't. He'll be happy finally to have a friend to confide in. Men need men friends to confide in, Harry. It's a law of nature."

"*I'll* beat you," I said.

"No, you won't," he said with a smile. "You'll be happy when I finally find out what happened to that wife of his. Why she broke Darian's poor, lonesome heart."

"Jarrett, I don't even want to know!"

"Oh, but you do, darling. You're simply dying to know, and so am I."

"Jarrett!"

But he was checking his watch. "We better go now, or we're going to be late."

"Jarrett!!"

But he picked up his Tom Ford jacket, gave me a wink, and walked out. "Are you coming, darling? We don't want to keep our clients waiting."

With an exasperated groan, I walked out after him. I knew Jarrett. Once he made up his mind to do something, it was impossible to talk him out of it. What had I done?!

CHAPTER 9

We arrived at a small concert hall in East London, where the first comeback concert of the Piquant Pack would be played. The girls were all there for rehearsals, and judging by the huge trucks parked outside, and people carting boxes of equipment inside, preparations were well underway.

"Isn't this a bit on the small side?" I asked Jarrett as he parked the Rolls right next to a limo that may or may not have been the girls' ride. "I would think the Piquant Pack would play Wembley Stadium or the Royal Albert Hall."

"They're starting small," said Jarrett knowingly. "This is just a tryout, darling. For a select audience. They want to see if they still got it—whatever 'it' is. You have to remember they haven't been on stage for twenty years, which is a very long time in the music industry. They all had to take voice lessons."

"Voice lessons?"

"Of course. The singing voice is like a muscle, Harry. If you don't work it, it atrophies and dies. Well, perhaps not dies, but it does lose power and pitch. Janell told me last night that when she tried to sing *Hungry* again, she simply couldn't!"

"You mean she forgot the lyrics?"

"Not the lyrics. Her voice. It was gone. She couldn't hit those high notes. Told me it's all about the breathing." He patted his belly. "Singing comes from here."

"The stomach?"

"The belly, Harry. It's about control. Control of your diaphragm. Hence the voice coach. Hence the small venue. They don't want to embarrass themselves."

"You know an awful lot about this, don't you?"

"Well, I have been a lifelong fan."

We entered the building, and found ourselves in the concert hall. People were all over the place, assembling the stage, the lighting gear, the sound system. It was impressive. "Wow," I said.

Jarrett smiled and spread his arms. "Welcome to my world, darling!"

I arched an eyebrow. "Your world? I didn't know you were a member of the Piquant Pack?"

"Well, I have been in show business all my life. I was on *Celebrity Big Brother*, remember? And I did have that episode with the boys of *One Dimension*."

"Right," I said dubiously. "That's still just the fringes, though. You were never actually on stage."

He looked hurt. "I was a rock star! I was on *Celebrity Big Brother*! How much bigger can the stage get?!"

"You were a rock star?"

"I was. When I heard that Queen were looking for a new lead singer, I decided to step in and fill the void that Freddie left. So I took some singing lessons and voila!"

"You were Queen's lead singer?" I asked dubiously.

"I... auditioned," he admitted. "No one ever sang a more

haunting rendition of *Somebody to Love* than me. Even Brian May had tears in his eyes. Actual tears."

I was pretty sure those tears had been tears of anguish at hearing that lovely music being mangled to such an extent. I'd heard Jarrett sing, and it wasn't pretty.

"And? Did they pick you?"

His face darkened. "They picked Adam Lambert over me. Can you believe it? The guy can barely carry a tune."

"I think he's got a great voice. He's a worthy successor to Freddie."

"Freddie would turn in his grave if he heard Adam Lambert." He frowned. "Maybe he does."

"You're just jealous," I said as we walked towards the stage. "Adam is super."

"See how little you know," he said acerbically, and crawled onto the stage.

We made our way into the wings, and then to the dressing rooms, where we found the five members of the Piquant Pack and... Darian.

"Darian!" I cried. "What are you doing here?"

"What does it look like he's doing?" asked Janell. "He's interrogating us!"

"Now, Miss Nodding," said Darian. "When the body of a murdered man is found, and that man claims to have been murdered by a certain individual, it's only proper procedure to interview that person in relation to that murder."

Janell's eyes were shooting fire. She did not look happy. "You promised," she reminded Darian.

"That was before Aldo Brookfield walked into Bethnal Green Police Station to file a murder charge against you."

Janell was seated in front of a vanity mirror, the other women huddled around her. There was no one else in the room, and I quickly closed the door to make sure we weren't overheard.

"I still don't understand how that's possible," said a wide-eyed Amaryllis.

"His soul must have occupied his dead body," said Carrie, "and carried it like a suit."

Perpetua shivered. "My gran told me that might happen when the amulet wasn't in place. She warned me never to remove the amulet." She sagged. "And now it has been."

"You mean he simply carried his own dead body around?" asked Courtney. "That sounds more like something from a horror movie."

"That's exactly what he did," said Janell. "Simply to make sure we got in trouble over his murder." She darted an angry look at Darian. "And you're helping him."

"I'm not helping anybody! I have to conduct a murder investigation. A charge was filed. A body has been found. A murder committed. I can't walk away from this. If I do, another inspector will simply pick up the case and then you'll be in a lot more trouble."

Janell frowned. "What do you mean? You're going to let this slide?"

"I'm going to interview the five of you, and then I'm going to do some more digging around, and when I finally file my report, I'm going to announce that the killer might never be found—which isn't that unusual for a murder that happened two decades ago."

Amaryllis cried out jubilantly, and threw herself around Darian's neck. "I knew it! You're such a sweetheart, Darian!" And then she kissed him full on the lips.

The other women soon followed suit, all hugging and kissing Darian until his face was covered in lipstick. I should have felt a pang of jealousy, but didn't. Instead, I was happy for the five women. Darian was right. If anyone else had taken charge of this investigation, they would have been in big trouble.

"Thanks, Darian," I breathed when the kissing was over, and gave him a kiss myself.

"This is the first time this has happened to me during a murder investigation," he finally said, looking a little frazzled.

I laughed, and wiped at his face with the sleeve of my shirt. "You might want to clean up before you head back to the station. You look like you were ambushed by the Spice Girls."

"Better," said Janell with a grin. "He was ambushed by the Piquant Pack."

"So, Darian," said Jarrett, taking a seat and directing a keen look at me. "If you have a moment, I would like to have a beer with you."

"A beer?" asked Darian, wiping the lipstick off his face. "You want us to have a beer?"

"Or a Coke Zero, in my case." He clapped the inspector on the back. "You and I go way back, don't we?"

"We've known each other exactly three months, Jarrett," said Darian.

Jarrett smiled. "It warms my heart that you're keeping track."

"I'm not. I met you when I met Harry. That's what I'm keeping track of."

"Oh," said Jarrett, his exuberance waning slightly. But then he trudged on. The Zephyr-Thorntons are nothing if not persistent. "Seeing as we're bosom buddies now, I think it's time we took our friendship to the pub. What say you, Inspector Watley?"

"If you hadn't noticed, I'm working, Jarrett," said Darian.

"I insist," Jarrett said with a stilted smile.

Darian stared at the billionaire's son for all of ten seconds, and finally said, "Fine. Let's hit the pub. Harry, are you game?"

"Harry's not coming. It's just you and me. Two rugged men. Celebrating their... mendom."

"Perhaps you mean manhood?" Darian asked.

"No, I would never share my manhood with you," said Jarrett with a laugh. "I reserve that particular pleasure for Deshawn. I'm touched by the compliment, though."

"I didn't mean..."

"Just let it go, Darian," I suggested. It was exactly what I'd been telling myself for the past five minutes, all throughout the painfully awkward conversation. There was no point in trying to stop Jarrett from making a mess of things, so I was resigned to bearing it with fortitude and hoping Darian would follow my lead.

Darian sidled up to me. "What's going on with Jarrett?" he whispered.

"He wants to ask you a few personal questions," I whispered back.

His eyebrows shot up. "Why?"

"Because he feels that I failed him in that department. He wants to ask you the 'hard' questions."

He looked positively uncomfortable now. "And what 'hard' questions would those be, exactly?"

I hesitated, then finally decided the cat was out of the bag. Jarrett had let it out. "He wants to know about your wife, Darian. He wants to know why she left you."

He stared at me. "My... wife?"

My cheeks were flushed as mortification rendered me mum.

"Look, if you wanted to know about Isabelle all you had to do was ask, Harry."

I nodded. I'd always felt it wasn't my place to ask, so I never had. "Tilda told me how she left you, and how... devastated you were. She also told me you never talked about it. I didn't want to pry, Darian. I really didn't. So..."

My voice trailed off as I gazed up at him with a look of apology.

"Tilda told you that?"

Tilda Fret was one of Darian's colleagues. I actually suspected she fancied the handsome inspector herself, though she'd never admit it.

Darian stood eyeing me for a long time, then finally said, "Isabelle didn't leave me, Harry. She died. Fifteen years ago."

"Oh, my God," I said, clasping my hands to my face. "I'm- I'm so sorry."

"I should have told you a long time ago. I guess… the wound is still a little raw. Even after all those years. Isabelle…" His voice trailed off, and I could see the pain reflected in his eyes.

"You don't have to talk about it," I assured him, taking his hands in mine. "It's just Jarrett with his dumb ideas. I couldn't stop him. He feels we should get married and…" Oh, God. I was just putting one foot after another in my mouth today, wasn't I? "I mean, not that I want to… Or actually maybe I do." I closed my eyes. This was a disaster!

He tilted up my chin and said softly, "Harry." I opened my eyes and found myself gazing into his gray peepers. The steely look was gone and replaced by a tender glint.

"I'm sorry, Darian," I said. "Forget what I just said. Forget everything."

"I want to talk about Isabelle. I just didn't want to jinx what we have by dragging up the ghosts of my past. Also, I didn't think you'd be interested."

"Oh, but I am interested," I assured him. "I want to know all about you, Darian."

He smiled. "Let's not do this here. Let's talk about this tonight, all right?"

"At the pub over drinks with Jarrett?"

He laughed. "Please, God, no!"

CHAPTER 10

While Darian interviewed the other members of the Piquant Pack, Jarrett and I left the dressing room to inspect the stage. Thinking back to what had happened at the Graham Norton Show last night, I wasn't sure Aldo wouldn't try another stunt, especially if Darian refused to arrest the five women, like Aldo had obviously intended.

"I think he's going to be furious when he discovers his little plan backfired," I told Jarrett.

"I think it's fine," Jarrett assured me. "What can he do? He's just a lonely old ghost."

"Lonely old ghosts can wreak a lot of havoc," I reminded him.

He gulped slightly. "So how do we handle this? How do we handle Aldo?"

I shook my head. Frankly, I was feeling a little out of my depth right then. The ghosts we'd encountered in the past had all been victims of crimes committed. They'd stuck around because they were incapable of moving on as long as their killers hadn't been apprehended. Once that happened, they were very happy to leave this mortal coil.

Aldo Brookfield was a different beast altogether. He, too, was the victim of a crime. But he wasn't going to move anywhere as long as the Piquant Pack weren't languishing in prison or worse. So we found ourselves in a completely different situation.

"I think we might need some assistance on this one," I said.

"I think you're right," Jarrett intimated.

We'd walked onto the stage and I found myself looking out into the concert hall. It wasn't Wembley, but it was still very impressive. "I can't imagine standing here in front of thousands of people," I said. "That must be such an incredible experience."

"It is," Jarrett assured me.

I turned to him. "You've performed live in front of an audience?"

"Of course. Though not as a rock singer. I played a tree in the high school play. A very sturdy oak," he added indignantly when I laughed.

"And before thousands of people?"

"Well, maybe not thousands, though it definitely felt like it."

We both gazed into the large arena. "We need Buckley, Jarrett."

"Well, where is he?"

"I don't know. But without him, we're sunk."

At that moment, Darian joined us onstage, tucking away his notebook. "I've interviewed the witnesses," he said, adopting his inspector voice.

"And?" I asked.

"They saw nothing, heard nothing, and know nothing. Their best guess? Aldo spent the night at some brothel, as was his habit, and got into a fight with some underworld figures, possibly in regards to a drug deal gone wrong. The thugs beat him up, killed him, and dumped his body. Which is exactly what I'm going to write in my report."

"Good for you," I said, patting his shoulder.

"Yes, I am rather proud of myself," he said genially, rocking back on his heels.

Just then, there was a roar of rage, and something streaked from overhead and knocked Darian sideways.

"Hey!" he cried.

"You screwed me over!" a voice sounded, and when I looked closer, I saw the ghost of Aldo materializing. He looked exactly the way he'd been twenty years ago: a jolly, fat man with florid features and beady little eyes, a cruel expression on his face. One side of his head was bashed in, where the Piquant Pack had had a whack at him, but apart from that, he looked a lot better than his remains had, at least according to Darian's description.

"You were supposed to arrest those five!" Aldo screamed.

Darian tried to get up, but Aldo knocked him back down.

"You're in cahoots with them, you piece of double-crossing flatfoot!"

"I'm not in cahoots with anyone," said Darian, once again trying to rise to his feet. But once more, Aldo rammed into him, slamming him over. "I'm going to get you for this," the dead manager hissed. "In fact I'm going to get all of you for this!"

"I suggest you leave my friends alone," a quiet voice suddenly sounded out of nowhere. When I looked up, I saw Buckley had finally joined us.

"And who are you?" asked Aldo nastily.

"I'm Sir Geoffrey Buckley and these are my friends. And you would be wise to leave them in peace."

"I'll show you wise!" screamed Aldo, and rushed the aged antiquarian.

I'd never seen two ghosts going head to head before, and wondered how that would play out. I wasn't disappointed. A storm seemed to rumble inside the concert hall, and flashes of lightning lashed the podium as Aldo and Buckley battled it out. Blows were exchanged, the impact like the crackling of an electrical storm, and for a moment I fully expected Thor to show up and join the fray. But then Aldo, realizing he wasn't going to be able to defeat Buckley, hollered, "Mark my words! You're all going to die!" And then, as suddenly as he'd appeared, he was gone, in a puff of smoke.

A sudden whoosh of air knocked us all flat on our asses. Then, silence.

"Phew," said Buckley. "That was one very nasty ghostie."

"That was Aldo Brookfield," I said.

"I know who he is," said Buckley with a smile as he descended to the stage.

Buckley is a kindly old gentleman with a lot of frizzy white hair. His costume was tailored by the finest Savile Row tailor, and even now, in death, he looks like a million bucks.

"Where were you, Buckley?" asked Jarrett. "We needed you."

"Oh, down at the racetrack," said Buckley airily. "I've discovered a neat new trick. Did you know that ghosts can actually inhabit a human body? I didn't! I've had a whale of a time jumping in and out of bodies. I actually inhabited the body of the Mayor of London for the past twenty-four hours. So much fun to be had!"

I couldn't blame Buckley for having a bit of fun. The life of a ghost was a little bit tedious, after all. And if this kept him on this side of the veil, helping us out, I was all for it. Though the Mayor of London? "Really, Buckley?" I asked. "You didn't do any damage, did you?"

"Oh, no. I just nudged him to try and discourage foreign investors from buying up all of London's prime real estate, driving hard-working Londoners out of home and hearth."

"Buckley!" I said. "I didn't take you for a socialist."

"These days it's very hard not to be a socialist," said Buckley, casting a cheerful eye at Jarrett, the most decidedly unsocialist person there.

"I'm also a socialist," Jarrett announced. "If it were up to me, all fat cats would be strung up from the highest tree, their wealth redistributed amongst the masses. Blood would flow in the streets, whether red or blue, and the cry would ring out, 'Down with the capitalist scum!'"

"That would mean you'd be strung up from the highest tree, too," said Darian, still recovering from his recent bout with the ghost of Aldo.

"I would gladly sacrifice myself for the cause," Jarrett announced.

"That's very noble of you, Jarrett," I said, "but I doubt whether it will ever come to that."

"Too true," sighed Sir Buckley sadly.

"So what are we going to do about Aldo?" I asked.

"No idea, Harry," said Buckley. "But you'll have to do something, as I have the distinct impression he'll be back—and this time he's not going to take prisoners."

"You mean you didn't vanquish him just now?" asked Jarrett, aghast.

"I merely drove him away. Ghosts cannot vanquish other ghosts, Jarrett."

"But… what if we equip you with some kind of weapon?"

"It doesn't work like that, I'm afraid."

"So there's no way to get rid of that horrible manager?"

"Oh, I'm sure there is a way," said Buckley. "But I'm sure I don't know what it is." He thought for a moment. "Let me ask around. The ghost community is surprisingly sociable. I think I've made more friends now than when I was still alive. Someone somewhere must know something." And with these words, he flew off, disappearing through the ceiling.

"So what happens now?" I asked.

"Now I report back to my superiors, announcing that the Piquant Pack are definitely innocent in the murder of their manager," said Darian, dusting himself off.

"And we will keep an eye on the girls," said Jarrett. "Make sure that ghostie doesn't return to try any funny business."

I nodded, even though I was pretty sure that even if Aldo returned, there wasn't much we could do to stop him. I gazed up at the ceiling, where Buckley had disappeared. My former employer was the only one who could help us. I hoped he wouldn't be long.

CHAPTER 11

"*Hungry! We're so hungry! Hungry for you—doo-bi-doo-bi-doo.*"

If the five women had had voice trouble before, they'd overcome it. They sang their biggest hit as well as they had twenty years before, even though I had to take Jarrett's word for it. I'd heard the song, of course, but had never paid much attention to it. I was more into contemporary pop music. Still, it was hard not to be lifted up by the sheer enthusiasm of the crowd going wild over the Piquant Pack. The energy was simply infectious, and I caught myself clapping and cheering along with the rest of them.

We were watching from the wings, Jarrett and I, while the ladies were rocking the stage. They were dressed in provocative outfits: chiffon dresses in their own colors: black, blond, red, blue and pink, and looked absolutely fabulous. We were twenty minutes into the concert, and so far so good. No strange voices booming from the sky. No lightning bolts striking the stage. And no dead managers uttering death threats.

"Aren't they the best?!" Jarrett yelled. "I just love them so much!"

"I wouldn't have pegged you for a Piquant Pack fan. More an ABBA fan. Or Barbra Streisand?"

"Oh, you're pulling out all the clichés now, are you? Keep going!"

"Cher? Madonna? Lady Gaga? Liza Minelli? Am I wrong?"

"Yes, you're so wrong!" he yelled over the noise. "So, so wrong!"

"So what do you like, apart from the Piquant Pack?"

"For your information, I defy all expectations and conventions. I like the Pet Shop Boys, Backstreet Boys, Vengaboys... Heck, I like all the boys!"

I laughed. "Of course you do!"

"I refuse to be a walking cliché, Harry! I simply refuse!"

"Trust me, Jarrett. You'll never be a cliché."

"Oh, God, I hope not," he said as he wiggled his butt to the music.

We watched for half an hour more, as the ladies took us through a selection of their hit songs from two decades ago. And just when I thought Buckley had been wrong and Aldo had given up his quest for vengeance, suddenly there was a loud clanking sound coming from somewhere up above. We all looked up, and that's when I saw it: the entire lighting construction, weighing a ton, had come unrigged, and was barreling down onto the stage, aimed for the five singers!

"Look out!" I cried, but luckily the girls had also spotted the impending disaster, and managed to dive out of the way, just as the heavy steel beams hit the stage with a deafening bang. The lights splintered on impact, showering us all in glass shards, and popping and exploding as they were knocked out by the power of the crash.

The music had stopped and a loud cackling sound could

be heard. "I'll get you!" the voice screamed. "I'll keep coming until you're all dead—each and every one of you!"

Jarrett and I got up, feeling dazed, and made our way to the five women, who'd been knocked back. "Are you all right?" I asked when I saw that Janell was covered in blood.

"Just some scrapes and bruises," she said as she got up with a groan. "What about the others?"

"I'm fine," announced Carrie, and one by one, the other ladies announced they'd survived this latest attack.

The crowd, which had witnessed the disaster, reacted remarkably well. There was no full-blown panic, and as people were herded towards the nearest exit by the security personnel on site, it became clear that whatever damage had been done wasn't physical but reputational.

"This is a disaster," said Janell as she picked glass shards from her dress. "This was supposed to be our big comeback. And now look what happened."

"I'm sure people will understand when you tell them it was a technical issue," I said.

"You think they'll believe that?"

"I'm sure they will."

"What about Aldo's message?"

"I'm sure the majority was too busy being shocked by the falling lights to take any notice," I said. "And if they did, they probably thought it was some joker."

"Some joker," Courtney grumbled. "He almost killed us. Twice now."

Amaryllis looked at me imploringly. "You have to help us, Harry. You have to save us from this crazy man. Next time he might succeed and kill us!"

I locked eyes with Jarrett, who nodded. "Why don't you all come with me," he suggested. "I'll put you up in my suite. That way we'll be in a better position to keep an eye on you and protect you."

"You have a suite?" asked Perpetua curiously.

"Yes, at the Ritz-Carlton. It's where I live, actually. And there's plenty of space for all of you. And you, of course, Harry," he added with a concerned look at me.

I knew what he meant. This Aldo wasn't merely going after his five former protégées, he was coming for us now as well.

"We have to talk to Buckley," I said. "He's the only one who can help us right now." The Wraith Wranglers had been outwrangled.

CHAPTER 12

"Maybe you should get in touch with Brian," Jarrett suggested. "Or that other guy. Peverell Wardop? At least they should be able to tell us what's going on."

Brian Rutherford was the one who'd started the Wraith Wranglers. If anyone would be able to tell us how to proceed, it was him. And Peverell was Brian's old boss, a ghost himself now, and had helped us out on our very first ghost haunting case. "I'll call him," I promised. "Though last time we spoke, he said he was dialing back on the Wraith Wranglers. Said things had gotten out of hand and he was focusing on the business side of the Wardop Group. Apparently some of the board members had gotten wise to these extracurricular activities of their president and they didn't approve."

"Shareholders," said Jarrett, clucking his tongue. "Always stirring up trouble."

I couldn't imagine Jarrett ever having trouble with shareholders. He never even went into the office, leaving all the work to his father, the real billionaire in the family.

"Basically it means we're on our own," I said. Without

Brian or Peverell to help us, it was up to us to get us out of this situation.

The five ladies had settled into their respective rooms, and the oohs and aahs told me they were pleased with their new lodgings. Jarrett's suite is quite a bit bigger than my own modest apartment. In fact my entire flat would fit snugly inside Jarrett's kitchen. Apart from his and Deshawn's bedrooms, there were four more rooms, and two bathrooms, to put up the guests. I had stayed here on occasion, and accommodations were more than adequate, which was to be expected from a five-star establishment like the Ritz.

Jarrett wandered from room to room, like the conscientious host he was, making sure his five guests were all comfortable. The idea was that if we all stuck together, Aldo would have much less of a chance to get at us. In theory this sounded great, but it didn't do much to make me feel more at ease. The women, though, seemed to like the notion.

"This is so great!" cried Amaryllis, jumping up and down on the bed. "I love this place!"

"I'm glad you like it," said Jarrett graciously. "And if there's anything you need, Deshawn is only one room away. Oh, and Grace, of course."

"Who's Grace?" asked Amaryllis.

"She's Jarrett and Deshawn's housekeeper," I explained.

"It's an interesting story," said Jarrett. "Grace played Maggie Smith's stunt double in the Harry Potter movies. Unfortunately her scenes never made it past the final cut. You should ask her sometime. It's a great story."

We moved to the next room, where Janell was putting her stuff away in the drawers. Like the others, this room had a hardwood floor, faux-marble columns, an actual chandelier, French windows leading to a small balcony that offered a great view of London, and a four-poster bed.

"This is so nice of you, Jarrett," said Janell, looking up. She looked a little pale, I thought, her usually so vibrant red hair having lost some of its luster. Well, that was not surprising, considering what she'd been through.

"It's an honor, really," said Jarrett. "I've been a Piquant Pack fan for so long this is like a dream come true."

"You know, I'm a fan of yours, too," said Janell. "I loved you in *Celebrity Salon*. The way you bleached Geri Halliwell's hair—that was such a fun moment!"

Jarrett smiled. "She wasn't too happy about that."

"Well, I thought you did a great job." She glanced up at him. "In fact, if you wanted to, you could do my hair anytime you like."

Jarrett clasped his hands together with glee. "I would love that!"

"It's a date," said Janell.

"Oh, you're on, sister," Jarrett chuckled happily. "In fact I'll do all your hair. We'll make it a fun girls night."

"You're not a girl, Jarrett," I reminded him.

"I'm an honorary girl," he said.

That, he most certainly was.

We moved to the next room, where Carrie had opened the window and was out on the balcony, gazing down at the busy street below. When we joined her, I could see red double-decker buses moving up and down the street, along with black cabs. From where we stood, they looked like tiny ants moving about.

"I'm so glad you're doing this, Jarrett," she said in that trademark raspy voice of hers. "This is such a treat."

"Won't your family be worried about you?" I asked.

She shook her head, her blue tresses swishing pleasantly. "I don't have a family." She looked away. "When the Piquant Pack split, I started a solo career. I always figured I'd have plenty of time for a family later—once my career had taken off again. But it never did, and when I finally started looking around for a decent bloke to share my life with, I discovered they were a lot harder to find than I'd imagined. I was in a few relationships, but nothing serious. Now I'm single, and have been for quite some time."

"You'll find someone," said Jarrett, the inveterate romantic. "And if you don't, I'll make sure you do. My matchmaking skills are legendary."

She laughed, her cheeks dimpling. "You're a real hoot, Jarrett."

"And you, my darling, are gorgeous. And don't let anyone tell you different."

"Thanks. And thanks for putting up with us. I know it can't be easy."

"Like I told Janell—it's a genuine honor," he said with a bow.

We moved to the next room, which had been Deshawn's before Jarrett had decided to give it away, and found Courtney staring at the flatscreen TV, furiously working the remote. "How does this frickin' thing work," she was muttering.

I saw that on the screen, *Brokeback Mountain* was playing, the scene where Heath Ledger and Jake Gyllenhaal were kissing and cuddling in their tent apparently stuck on repeat.

"Let me have that, darling," said Jarrett, snatching the remote from Courtney's fingers. He deftly clicked Heath and Jake away. "It's Deshawn's favorite movie at the moment," he explained. "He simply cannot get enough of it." He then channel-surfed until he landed on a commercial for *The Great British Bake Off*, where Deshawn's Bundt cake was once again disappearing into Paul Hollywood's face. "And we don't want that either," Jarrett said, furiously clicking the remote again.

"Hey, I like the Bake Off," said Courtney, quite surprisingly.

"No, you don't," said Jarrett.

"Yes, I do," she insisted. "Give me that remote." She reached for the little clicker, but Jarrett kept it out of reach. "Give me that!"

"Nobody is watching Paul Hollywood seduce *my* boyfriend under *my* roof!" Jarrett squealed, and yanked the remote away from Courtney's grabbing hands.

Mysteriously, the TV landed on BBC One, where a news item was being shown. It was the disastrous Piquant Pack concert, footage of the lighting gear crashing down on stage featured in slow motion.

"Oh, God," said Courtney. "So awful."

"You don't want to see that either," Jarrett decided. "Way too depressing." He finally landed on BBC Two, where Sir David Attenborough was explaining something about the mating rituals of mammals. "Now this is something you'll want to see," said Jarrett with decision. "Very instructive."

Courtney threw her head back, and laughed a booming laugh. "You're something else, aren't you, Jarrett!"

"Yes, I believe I am," said Jarrett. "And you better get used to it, Piquant Pink."

She eyed him with a humorous glint in her dark eyes. "I'm sure I will."

The next room housed Perpetua, who was just checking under the bed when we came upon her. "Looking for the ghost?" I asked. She sat up so quickly she bumped her head against the bed.

"Didn't anyone ever tell you not to sneak up on people?" she asked, massaging the injured spot.

"I'm sorry," I said. "I was just wondering what you were doing down there."

"Well, this room is so incredibly clean," she said, sitting down on the bedside carpet, "I almost can't believe it. Either you have an incredible housekeeper, or Deshawn is a fantastic cleaner on top of being a fantastic baker."

"We have a fantastic housekeeper," Jarrett said, "although Deshawn is pretty great himself."

"Can I steal your housekeeper away from you?" asked Perpetua. "A housekeeper who can keep an apartment this clean is worth her weight in gold."

"Ha!" Jarrett laughed. "You can snatch Grace away from us over our cold, dead bodies!"

Perpetua smiled. "Wait until you have kids. You'll appreciate her even more. At least if you get to keep her. We've been through a dozen housekeepers and have a hard time holding onto number thirteen at the moment."

"Oh, right. You're married with four kids, aren't you?" I asked.

"Harry," said Jarrett reproachfully. "Perpetua isn't merely married, she's the proud wife of none other than Brad Ultima, only the best soccer player this country has ever produced."

"Thanks," said Perpetua, batting her eyelashes bashfully. "Brad will love to hear that."

"What does he think about this whole Aldo Brookfield thing?" I asked.

"He doesn't know," said Perpetua. "This all happened long before we met, and since we all swore an oath never to tell anyone, I decided not to."

"Are you going to tell him now?" I asked.

She wavered. "I don't think so. It isn't something I'm particularly proud of, and if I do tell him, eventually the kids will find out, and I don't want them to know that their mummy has committed murder."

I nodded. "I understand. Though he might wonder what is going on."

"Oh, I just told him it's all part of the show. That's what I tell everybody. It's the story our publicist is spreading to the media as well. All part of the comeback strategy."

"Do you think they'll buy it?"

"Honey, they'll buy anything we sell them. What is the alternative? That the ghost of our dead manager has come back to haunt us? Nobody is going to believe that story."

She was right, of course. No one in their right mind would believe a story like that. Which was all for the best. We didn't want to draw any attention to what had happened twenty years ago. That was one part of the Pack's story that best stay buried.

We moved into the living room, and we'd just settled down in the plush couches, when Deshawn arrived. When he saw the five women walking in from their respective bedrooms, he blinked. "Um, do we have visitors, Jarrett?"

"Yes, we do, Deshawn," Jarrett announced. "You're not the only one who likes to hobnob with celebrities, you know. You have your Paul Hollywood, I have the Piquant Pack. Oh, and incidentally, I have given your room to Courtney—and don't give me that look. I've switched off *Brokeback Mountain*. She does not have to be made privy to your most intimate and most sordid fantasies."

"We were attacked again," I explained.

"Oh, my," said Deshawn, his face betraying his upset. "What happened?"

"If you spent less time playing celebrity baker, you would have noticed we almost died today, Deshawn," said Jarrett.

"Aldo dropped the lighting gear on our heads," said Janell, dropping down on the couch next to Jarrett. "We barely escaped with our lives."

"Oh, dear," said Deshawn, looking positively horrified.

"It's not your fault, Deshawn," I said.

"Even so, I should have been there."

"It's fine," said Amaryllis softly. "There was nothing you could have done."

"So what happens now?" asked Perpetua.

"Now we wait," I said.

Courtney raised an eyebrow. "Wait for what? For Aldo to strike again?"

"We wait for Buckley," I explained. "He's going to come up with a plan." At least that's what I hoped.

"We trust you, Harry," said Carrie. "We know you'll protect us from this maniac."

Her words were touching, and I envied her a confidence I wasn't feeling myself. And judging from the looks on Jarrett and Deshawn's faces, they weren't either.

CHAPTER 13

I'd expected the Piquant Pack to turn in early, after the harrowing day they'd had, but I was wrong. On the contrary, they seemed reluctant to return to their respective rooms, and preferred to hang around the living room, safe in each other's company. It was almost like a slumber party, without the pillow fights. There was food, though. Plenty of food. Deshawn, still in full Bake Off mode, decided to have one more go at the pièce de résistance he intended to create for the show: a fruity sponge cake.

"We'll all pitch in," said Janell enthusiastically when she got wind of Deshawn's plans. She got up from the white leather couch she'd been lounging on and followed Deshawn into the kitchen.

"Oh, do we really have to?" asked Courtney, who was lazing about with her iPad, checking the news reports on the girls' comeback tour. "Why don't you guys bake the cake, and I'll eat it. I'll play Mary Berry's part and do the tasting, all right?"

"And we'll be the jury members," said Amaryllis with a giggle, hooking her arm through Carrie's.

"So who's doing Paul Hollywood?" asked Perpetua.

All eyes turned to Jarrett, who held up a limp-wristed hand. "Don't look at me, darlings. If anyone is doing Paul it's Deshawn."

"No, he's not," said Carrie. "Deshawn is the candidate."

"So he says," Jarrett muttered.

"Where's that good-looking cop?" asked Courtney. "He'd make a wonderful Paul Hollywood. Minus the amazing blue eyes, of course."

"That good-looking cop you're referring to happens to be Harry's boyfriend," said Jarrett.

"Oh, we know that," said Amaryllis with a cheeky giggle. "Lucky you, Harry!"

"Thanks," I said with a grin. "Though we haven't been together all that long."

"I've seen the two of you together," said Courtney. "You're definitely mating material."

It was obvious she'd been watching that David Attenborough documentary very carefully.

"Are you going to get married?" asked Carrie, fixing me with an intent look.

"Well, I don't know about that," I said. "He hasn't asked me yet at any rate."

"Oh, but he will," Jarrett said. "I'm sure about it. And if he doesn't, I will."

"You will ask him to marry you?" asked Amaryllis. "But I thought you and Deshawn were a thing?"

"Deshawn and I are a thing," Jarrett confirmed. "All I meant was that if Darian neglects to go down on one knee, I'll make sure that he does. I'll be his wedding proposal coach."

"Is that a thing?" asked Amaryllis, screwing up her face into an expression of confusion.

"It most certainly is," Jarrett confirmed. "A lot of men

have no idea how to go about proposing to a woman. They need someone to hold their hand and show them the way. I'm that man."

"No, you're not," I said. "Give me one couple you've coached."

"I've coached myself," said Jarrett, raising his chin. "And quite successfully."

"That doesn't count!" said Courtney, laughing. "You can't coach yourself."

"I can, too," Jarrett insisted stubbornly. "Just ask Deshawn. He was swept off his feet, which is the purpose of any wedding proposal."

"Hey, you guys," Janell said, walking in from the kitchen. "I thought we were going to help Deshawn bake his sponge cake? Chop-chop," she added, clapping her hands.

With a groan, Courtney got up off the couch and stretched. She was the tallest one of the five, and the most muscular one as well. I wouldn't like to meet her in a dark alley after midnight. Carrie jumped to her feet with a pantherine litheness. Together, they followed Janell into the kitchen.

Amaryllis, who'd curled up on the couch, batted her eyelashes at me. "Do I have to come? It's so comfy here."

"No, you don't have to come," I said. "As long as you're here, you can do whatever you like. Isn't that right, Jarrett?"

"Sure," said Jarrett absentmindedly. Something on his phone had drawn his attention, and when I leaned in to have a look, he muttered, "Will you look at this."

It was the cover of *The Sun*, England's most popular tabloid, and it read, 'Piquant Spooky.' A blurry picture of a humanoid figure accompanied the headline. The figure appeared to unfasten the cables that held up the lighting gear. I recognized the ghostly apparition as Aldo Brookfield.

"That didn't take long," I said.

"I know. Pretty soon they'll make the connection to Aldo."

He gestured at a smaller article, which recounted the strange reappearance of Aldo at the police station, before expiring on the floor, dead. There was also a wild story by an officer named Donnie Ricard, who claimed that the man was one of the walking dead, and had already expired before he walked into the police station.

"It won't be long before they put two and two together and start speculating about the girls' role in Aldo's disappearance," said Jarrett.

"Which means we don't have a lot of time to make Aldo disappear again."

We shared a look of concern. Aldo's reappearance had had the effect he'd been looking for. Soon people would start asking questions about the Piquant Pack, and Darian would have no other choice than to haul them in for questioning, and then it would only be a matter of time before the tabloids found them guilty, even if the police didn't.

We walked into the kitchen, where Deshawn and Janell were baking up a storm. The butcher block was stocked with ingredients and Deshawn, a smudge of flour on his brow, was handling a rolling pin with precision, preparing the cake base.

The other girls were all seated around the island, perched on high stools, aiding with the various tasks that went into baking the perfect cake.

"Remember that on the day of the shoot you'll have to do this all by yourself, Deshawn," said Jarrett, looking on a little peevishly.

"I'm well aware of that, Jarrett," said Deshawn. His cheeks were flushed, but he'd lost none of his trademark equanimity. If anyone could stay calm and collected under fire, it was definitely Deshawn.

"Maybe we shouldn't help him then," said Courtney, who

had dropped her head on her arms and was staring morosely at the proceedings. I guessed she wasn't much of a baker. "I mean, if we do all the work, he won't be prepared for the crucible of the Great Bake Off."

"We do all the work?" asked Janell. "I do all the work, you mean."

"You, we... it's all the same," said Courtney with a shrug. "We're the five musketeers, remember. One for all and all for one."

Janell planted a hand on her hip, a cloud of flour wafting up. "Seems to me that it's one for all today. Aren't you going to pitch in?"

"Yes, Court," said Amaryllis. "Show us your baking prowess."

"Why don't you show me yours?" Courtney threw right back.

"I can't bake," said Amaryllis sadly. "Though I would love to learn."

"Well, now's your chance," said Carrie. "Deshawn will teach you everything you need to know."

"Oh, will you, Deshawn?" asked Amaryllis, clutching at Deshawn's arm, causing him to chop off a piece of his cake base.

He winced slightly, then said, "Of course I will. It'll be my pleasure."

Jarrett was casting nasty glances at his fiancé, and it was obvious love did not live here anymore, or at least it didn't now. "Don't compliment him too much," he said. "We don't want him to become too big for his britches. Soon he'll be intolerable."

"Oh, but Deshawn can never be intolerable," said Perpetua, sidling up to the baking prodigy. She mussed up the man's hair. "He's simply the cutest—aren't you, Deshawn?"

"Thanks," said Deshawn, unperturbed by all this female attention.

"He is the perfect man," gushed Carrie. "Too bad you're not into women, Deshawn. I would fancy you."

"Me too," said Amaryllis with a giggle. "I'd fancy Deshawn so much."

"I'd marry Deshawn in a heartbeat," Janell agreed. "What's not to like? He's kind, handsome, sweet, respectful, an amazing cook, and probably great in bed, too."

"Is that true, Deshawn?" asked Perpetua. "Are you great in bed?"

"I aim to give satisfaction, Miss," said Deshawn phlegmatically.

"Ooh, Deshawn," breathed Courtney. "That's the sexiest thing I ever heard."

"Yes, can you repeat that, Deshawn?" asked Carrie, rubbing the man's arm.

"I endeavor to give satisfaction," said Deshawn, incrementally raising an eyebrow.

"Deshawn!" moaned Amaryllis. "You certainly satisfy me!"

Soon, the five members of the Piquant Pack were all over Deshawn, who took it in his stride, doing his best to focus on his cake and not the attention being lavished upon him by the most popular girl band of the nineties.

Jarrett watched it all with rising indignation, and finally heaved a disgusted snort and stalked out of the kitchen. The budding wedding proposal coach seemed to be having second thoughts about Deshawn being the love of his life.

CHAPTER 14

After enjoying a late dinner—and Deshawn's cake, of course—the girls finally turned in for the night. Jarrett, Deshawn and I lingered in the kitchen, discussing what to do next. Deshawn was putting glasses, cups, saucers and dishes into the dishwasher, ahead of Grace who usually came in in the morning to finish cleaning up.

I'd finally called Brian Rutherford but unfortunately he was unable to help us. Ghost hunting had been something he was keenly interested in when he got his start at the Wardop Group, but the board of directors had recently shut him down. It appeared that even when you were the president of one of the most successful companies on the face of the planet, there was only so much you could do. When I asked if Peverell was available, he said the founder of the Wardop Group had decided he needed to focus on his company's bottom line and not the idle pursuit of ghosts.

Looked like we were on our own. And we'd gone back and forth on how to defeat this raging ghost, when finally Buckley joined us.

"Oh, Buckley," I said. "Am I glad to see you." Judging from

the triumphant look on the antiquarian's face, he'd found something. "Please tell me you have a solution. Anything."

"Yes, I have," he announced, barely able to contain his delight.

"Well, what is it?" asked Jarrett, who was still in a foul mood after the outrageous display of affection his favorite girl band had lavished upon his boyfriend.

"The thing is, Aldo Brookfield's ghost isn't your average run-of-the-mill ghostie," said Buckley. "The man was a predator in life, and he remains a predator in death. He'll do anything to linger on this shore and hurt the people he feels wronged him. He has, for all intents and purposes, turned into a ghoul."

"Yes, yes, we all know the man is a pest," said Jarrett. "Get on with it, will you? How do we get rid of the horrible nuisance and defeat him once and for all?"

"A ghoul," I said pensively. "What does that mean?"

"It means he's a very bad man," said Jarrett. "What do you think it means?"

"It means his single purpose now is to cause damage," said Buckley. "It also means he can't be reasoned with. He's not going to listen to anyone. In fact, the more you try to reason with him, the angrier he will become, and consider you his enemy."

"And then he'll try to hurt us, too," I concluded.

"Exactly."

"So what do we do?" asked Deshawn, taking a seat at the kitchen table.

"We consult a specialist," said Buckley. "And I know just the right one."

"A specialist? But we're supposed to be the specialists," said Jarrett. "We're selling our services to the Piquant Pack."

"It's obvious we're in way over our heads here, Jarrett," I said. "We need help."

"I talked to a few colleagues—fellow ghosts who like to hang out at the racetrack—and they all told me the same thing. There's only one person with sufficient knowledge to root out a ghoul and that's Evette Gorina."

"Who?" asked Jarrett with a frown.

"Evette Gorina," Buckley repeated. "She works as a psychic in the East End. She has her own shop. Tarot cards, crystals, fortune telling, that sort of thing. But she's also a very powerful ghost hunter."

"Then why haven't we heard of her before?" asked Jarrett. "If she's so great, why haven't we met her at some ghost hunters convention?"

"We've only been doing this for a very short time, Jarrett," I reminded him. "There might be dozens of very able and capable ghost hunters out there that we've never met."

"And it's not as if there are conventions for ghost hunters," Deshawn chimed in.

"Well, there certainly should be," Jarrett said. "It would be fun to mingle."

"Did you check out this Evette?" I asked Buckley.

"Of course," he said. "I wouldn't be much of a ghostly assistant if I hadn't, would I?"

"Oh, is that your title now?" asked Jarrett. "Ghost assistant?"

"Jarrett," I admonished him. "Be nice to Buckley. He's the only one who can help us defeat Aldo and save us from a fate worse than death."

Jarrett grumbled something under his breath.

"I went to check out this woman's shop and she appears genuine. While I was there, she was reading a woman's fortune, and I had only been inside the shop for five minutes when she not only acknowledged my presence, but told me that I was being hunted by a very powerful and very evil force. When I asked her if she knew of a way to defeat this force, she told me that she did, and asked me to convey the message to you that you will only overcome this dark time if you all stick together."

"Stick together?" I asked.

Buckley nodded his ghostly head and gave Deshawn's cake an eager look. One of the drawbacks of being a ghost is that certain physical pleasures are a thing of the past, like snacking on cake, or smoking a cigarette, or getting an alcohol buzz. "She said Aldo is trying to break up the Wraith Wranglers. Cause a rift. You will only defeat him if you work together as a team."

I glanced at Jarrett and he looked away. Perhaps this Evette was right. Jarrett had made quite a nuisance of himself lately, so much so he was even starting to piss me off, not to mention Deshawn. Could this be the work of Aldo? Trying to break up the band?

"Look, I don't know about this so-called specialist," said Jarrett. "But I feel that we simply don't need her. I mean, what can she tell us that we don't know already? We know Aldo Brookfield is a very bad man. We know he's coming after the girls and after us. And we know we have to defeat him. So is any of this even remotely helpful?"

"It's helpful if she knows how to defeat Aldo," I said. I turned to Buckley. "Can she teach us how to defeat a ghoul?"

Buckley smiled and cracked his ghostly knuckles. "Oh, yes, she can."

CHAPTER 15

The suite was quiet, a soft snoring the only sound that could be heard. Aldo roamed from room to room, rubbing his hands with glee. There they were, all his precious girls. They'd aged a bit, of course, but they were still highly delectable. He looked down at the sleeping form of Amaryllis, who'd always been his favorite. What a pity he was a ghost now, or he'd ravage that hot body, just like he had before they'd attacked and killed him.

He morphed with the wall and came out the other end, floating over Janell. She was the strong, fierce leader, the same way she'd always been. Her face looked so peaceful, asleep, but he knew better. There was always something going on behind those watchful and intelligent eyes. The way she used to look at him turned him on, even now. He chuckled freely as he imagined what he'd do to her. "Not much longer now, my pet," he whispered, touching her cheek with his finger. "Soon. Very soon."

She stirred in her sleep, and turned on her side.

He hovered into the next room, where he found Carrie asleep in her underwear. She'd thrown off the sheets, as usual. Carrie was a hot one, he thought with a grin. He lasciviously let his eyes roam across her lithe form. Still in great shape, he saw. Still the body of a kickboxer, which he'd experienced the night she'd kicked him in the gut. His smile evaporated as he thought back to that fateful night. The night his life had changed.

He drifted off into the painting of the Pet Shop Boys and came out the other side, finding himself directly over Courtney. She was still a strong girl, and, like the others, had been treated well by Father Time. They'd all taken very good care of themselves, which was gratifying to discover. He floated down and picked up an extra pillow, then moved it over Courtney's head, making to smother her. She'd been the one who'd dealt him the killing blow, and for that, she would be made to suffer. And as she coughed, he quickly removed the pillow again and replaced it on the bed.

Not now. Not yet. If he was going to do this, he'd take them out all at once. And make them hurt. Their deaths would be painful and protracted. He giggled as he drifted in to check up on Perpetua. He glanced at the picture frame placed next to the bed. It depicted Perpetua's husband, some famous soccer player he'd never heard of. And a gaggle of kids, of course. The corners of his lips turned down in an expression of disgust. To see his girl as a mother was an aberration. He found it absolutely disturbing.

With a flick of his finger, he tipped over the picture frame, hiding the gruesome reality that his girls had turned into women in his absence, and stared down at the still athletic form of the most stylish addition to the Piquant Pack. *His* Piquant Pack.

Finally, he moved into a room where two men slept, side by side. Another aberration, he thought bitterly. One was thickset and balding, the other thin and tall. They could be Laurel and Hardy, he thought with a disgusted grunt. He hated what he had to do next, but knowing it was the only way, he resigned himself to his fate, and promptly jumped into the fat one. He seemed to be a big hit with the girls, baking up a storm for their enjoyment. And as he adjusted himself to this new reality, he thought that life, even though it had thrown him a few curveballs, was finally going his way again.

※

Jarrett woke up in the middle of the night. He didn't know what had awakened him, so he blinked against the darkness of the room. Then he got it. Deshawn was asleep next to him. This was an unusual arrangement, as they usually occupied separate bedrooms. Now, since Jarrett had given his room away to Courtney, he'd had no other choice but to stay here. He glanced down at Deshawn's sleeping form, and suddenly had the distinct impression something was off about the man.

He roused the proud baker by stirring his shoulder. "Deshawn," he whispered.

"Mh…" Deshawn murmured, turning around to face him and twisting the sheet closer around his form. "What do you want?"

"Are you all right, darling?"

Deshawn's eyes opened, and Jarrett did a double take. His boyfriend's eyes looked different somehow. Almost… evil. "For your information, I was sleeping," Deshawn grumbled.

"I know. I was just… worried I guess."

"Worried about what?"

"That crack I made about Paul Hollywood and the Bake Off earlier? I'm sorry about that, darling," he said now. "I guess I'm simply jealous."

"No need to be jealous," said Deshawn. "Hollywood's just a blue-eyed fatso."

"Would you call Paul Hollywood fat? I think he looks just fine."

"He's fat," said Deshawn. "Just a big, fat bully. Now go to sleep."

"But I don't want to sleep, darling. Not just yet. Do you know we haven't talked in days? Not really talked, I mean. I've been bitching and moaning about that Bake Off ever since you entered the competition and you've borne it all with admirable imperturbability, but now I feel I owe you an apology."

Deshawn sighed. "Well, apologize already and get it over with, will you?"

He gave his future husband a pained look. "You don't have to be mean about it. I just said I'm jealous. Of the attention you get. Of the company you keep. It just seems to me that you're becoming a star, darling, and you're going to leave me behind."

"I'm not leaving you behind," said Deshawn with another mighty sigh. "Now can we go back to sleep?" He gestured at his face. "This beautiful visage doesn't maintain itself, you know. It needs a lot of rest."

"Oh," he cried. "You're so cruel!"

"You're cruel to keep me awake."

"Oh," he sniffed. "I knew it. This newfound fame has gone to your head." He reached out and touched Deshawn's arm. "Where is the wonderful man I met? Where is the kindhearted teddy bear I proposed to? Where is the real Deshawn? Is he still in there?"

"Of course the real Deshawn is still in there," Deshawn grunted. "Don't be daft, you silly poofter." And with these harsh words, he flipped over, turning his broad back on Jarrett, and promptly dozed off.

Jarrett bit his lip, tears springing to his eyes. "Deshawn," he whispered, reaching out a desperate hand. "Sweet, sweet Deshawn. Where have you gone?" Then he directed his eyes at the ceiling, raised his hands in dramatic fashion and cried in a tremulous voice, "Why?! Why?! Whyyyyyy!"

CHAPTER 16

The next morning I woke up to total pandemonium. I'd slept on the couch, as all the rooms were taken. Janell had offered to share her bed, but as I didn't want to inconvenience her, I'd kindly declined. Besides, sleeping on a couch in a suite at the Ritz-Carlton wasn't the same as sleeping on a couch back at my place. Jarrett's couch was more comfortable than my own bed, and I'd slept like a rose.

Now, however, it appeared as if a dozen people were all screaming at once. Which they were. The problem was the bathrooms, apparently. As there were only two of those available, and there were five women to contend each other over them, the argument had to be fought out at the top of their voices. Finally it was agreed that Perpetua and Amaryllis would go first, as they were both mothers—though I didn't see why that would be a factor—and also because Amaryllis was the baby of the company.

I rubbed my eyes and stretched out luxuriously. Perhaps I could ask Jarrett to let me stay here permanently? I watched as Perpetua and Amaryllis stalked into their respective bathrooms, and the fight that broke out amongst the three others over who got to go in after them.

"I'm the eldest," said Janell. "I should get first dibs."

"You should get last dibs. Since you're the eldest, you are pretty much beyond salvage anyway," said Courtney, very harshly, I felt.

"I'm not beyond salvage!" cried Janell. "I'm still beautiful."

"In an elderly way."

"You take that back, Court!"

"I'm not taking anything back. It's the truth and it deserves to be told."

"Oh, come off it, you fat cow," said Carrie. "You always were the nasty one."

"Nasty and proud, baby," said Courtney. "And who are you calling a fat cow, you stick figure?"

"Ladies, ladies," I said, deeming it necessary to intervene. "Can't you see this is Aldo's doing? He has you all at daggers drawn."

Courtney frowned at me. "But she called me fat."

"And she called me old."

"And she called me a stick figure."

"That's just Aldo's bad influence. Divide and conquer. Ring a bell?"

They stood scowling at one another, then finally Courtney said, "You're not that old, Janell. And you're kinda beautiful, I guess. In your own special way."

"And you're not so fat," said Carrie. "You gained some weight, but not all that much."

"And you may be thin, but at least you're healthy," said Courtney.

"Hugsies?" asked Janell.

The others nodded, and the embrace that followed even included little old me! And we were still hugging it out when the front door to the suite opened and a lady walked in who looked surprisingly a lot like Maggie Smith. When she saw four women with their arms around each other, she stiffened, and said in a disapproving tone, "Well!"

"Hey, Grace," I said. "Meet Courtney, Janell and Carrie. They're the Piquant Pack."

"I'm sure they are," said Grace, still with that disapproving look on her face. She peeled off her periwinkle velvet gloves and placed them on the hallway dresser, removed her coat and hat and nodded a greeting at the three women. "Pleased to make your acquaintance I'm sure. Guests of Jarrett and Deshawn I presume?"

"We are," said Janell. "And did anyone ever tell you that you're the spitting image of Maggie Smith?"

"No, you're the first one," said Grace acerbically.

"Oh, before you start, there are two more ladies occupying the bathrooms at the moment," I said. "And the kitchen is a mess. Deshawn was demonstrating his baking skills last night."

"Of course he was," she said primly. "At least there's one person making a living in this household." She raised her head and stalked off in the direction of the kitchen.

"She's a real treat, isn't she?" asked Courtney, staring after the housekeeper.

"Grace is an acquired taste," I agreed. "But she's a great housekeeper. In fact Jarrett and Deshawn wouldn't know what to do without her."

As if summoned by my words, at that moment Jarrett walked in out of his bedroom. He was dressed in a monogrammed gold-and-burgundy velvet housecoat and looked a little disheveled. He had bags under his eyes and his hair was a tousled mess.

"Jarrett," I said. "Grace is here."

"As was to be expected," he muttered, avoiding my eyes.

"Are you all right?" I asked.

"As all right as a man who's been jilted by his lover can be."

"Jilted by your lover? What do you mean?"

He raised his head. "I'm sure you're not interested in my sad stories, Harry. After all, your life is a bed of roses, isn't it? It reads almost like a fairy tale. Mine, on the other hand, is the stuff of nightmares."

"A billionaire's son, living at the Ritz-Carlton, enjoying the company of the Piquant Pack, having Maggie Smith herself clean up after him? You're right. That sounds like a real nightmare," I said.

A sob escaped his throat. "Oh, Harry," he said brokenly. "I'm so sorry. I've been a hound—a cad—a fiend! Can you please forgive me?"

I frowned at him. "What *is* going on with you this morning, Jarrett?"

"I told you! Deshawn was mean to me last night."

"That's impossible. Deshawn doesn't have a mean bone in his body."

"Well, then all the bones in his body have suddenly turned mean. Very, very mean."

At that moment, Deshawn walked in from the bedroom, humming a gay tune. "Good morning, ladies," he said with a flicker of interest in his eyes. "Aren't you a sight for sore eyes?"

"Thank you, Deshawn," said Courtney, moving over to the baking prodigy and wrapping her arms around him. "You're just the sweetest man alive, aren't you?"

He wrapped an equally eager arm around her, and when I saw his hand descend to the woman's firm buttocks, I raised an astonished eyebrow. Carrie and Janell also joined the early morning hugfest, and for a brief moment I thought Deshawn looked just like Hugh Hefner entertaining three Playmates at the Playboy Mansion. He was even fondling

Janell's boob when she slapped his hand away and said, "Naughty, naughty, Deshawn!"

They moved off in the direction of the parlor, and I exchanged a confused look with Jarrett. "What's going on with Deshawn?"

"It's that Bake Off!" Jarrett cried, plunking down on the couch. "The whole thing's gone to his head!"

"But... has it turned him straight?"

Jarrett shrugged. "I wouldn't be surprised. All this time I was thinking the danger emanated from Paul Hollywood, but now it's become quite clear to me the real danger is those women assistants! They're like catnip and Deshawn has suddenly decided he wants to be the cat!"

"Is that even possible?"

"It is! Gays get confused about their sexuality all the time. I just never thought it would happen to Desha-ha-ha-hawn!" He broke down.

I joined him on the couch, hugging and patting his back. And that's how Grace found us. She directed a scathing look at yet another hugging couple and tsk-tsked quietly.

CHAPTER 17

We'd arrived at a small shop in the East End. It was located in an ethnically mixed neighborhood, full of Chinese restaurants, Vietnamese snack bars, Congolese bars, and a variety of other food places representing the world's nations. The streets were milling with shoppers, taxis honking to cut through the crowds, and the scent of gasoline mingled with rotisserie chicken, old world spices, and the mustiness caused by a dreary, rainy day.

Jarrett glanced up at the overcast sky as he slammed the door to the Rolls. "Even God in his heaven is mourning."

"I'm sure God is merely sending some rain our way so the crops can grow."

"Why do you always have to be so prosaic? Is there no place for romance in your world, Harry?"

"There's plenty of romance in my world," I said. "Though my love interest is currently trying to solve the unsolvable murder of a perverted old manager."

"Oh, and how is that working out for him?"

"It's hard to solve a murder whose suspects you've sworn not to arrest."

"Right," he said vaguely, showcasing an increasing lack of interest in this case.

The shop where Evette Gorina plied her trade was a smallish affair, wedged in between a Chinese restaurant that featured a large dragon as its marquee, and a sex cinema that had seen better days—and a less Internet-embracing clientele. The little shop was called Magical Mages, which seemed like an unnecessary repetition. Then again, sometimes people need to be hit over the head with a thing to get the point.

The storefront was painted a flaming red with touches of yellow, and featured an Egyptian eye motif. The display window was filled with the usual tricks of the trades: tarot cards in all shapes and sizes, crystals and other healing stones in all manner of setting, and lots and lots of books, CDs and DVDs promoting tranquility, a healthy love life and enlightenment.

We stepped inside, a wind chime over the door tinkling pleasantly.

"Coming," a melodious voice announced from the heart of the store.

We both started perusing the various items on offer. I checked a display stand of earrings and bracelets while Jarrett inspected a collection of meditation pillows of bold Persian design. It didn't seem to catch his fancy as he gave them an annoyed kick. Still sore over Deshawn's sudden change of sexual inclination, I imagined.

A smallish woman dressed in a long, flowing kaftan with Eastern embroidery floated in from the back of the store and took up her position behind the counter. Her face was wreathed in so many wrinkles it was hard to guess her age. She might have been sixty or she might have been a hundred. Her pale blue eyes were twinkling, though, and her smile was warm and engaging. "How can I help you?" she asked.

"Don't you know already?" asked Jarrett nastily. "And you're supposed to be a psychic."

"Jarrett!" I hissed. "Show some respect."

He sighed, going through one of his mood swings again, his eyes growing moist. "I'm so sorry, Mrs. Mage. I'm going through a rough patch. My love life has suffered a debilitating blow and I don't know how to cope."

She smiled. "When all is said and done, young man, you'll find that it was all for the best."

"I'm afraid of that," he said. "I'm afraid Deshawn and I were never meant to be."

"And my name is not Mrs. Mage," she said amiably. "It's Evette Gorina."

"Of course it is."

With a critical eye at Jarrett, I said, "We're actually here for another matter entirely, Mrs. Gorina. The thing is…" I bit my lower lip anxiously. "Can we talk to you in private?"

"Of course," said the woman. "I have a small consultation room in the back. Will that be sufficient?"

I nodded, and we both followed the woman behind the counter and down a narrow corridor, painted in a very vivid green. She seemed to be fond of the bolder colors.

"Maybe I should ask her about Deshawn?" asked Jarrett.

"We have more important things to deal with first, Jarrett," I said a little reproachfully. "Like the ghoul that's trying to kill us and our clients?"

"Oh, right," he said, then shook his head. "I'm so sorry, Harry. I'm just a mess today."

"Just stop apologizing," I said. "And pull yourself together."

"I'll certainly try," he said doubtfully.

We'd arrived in the small room indicated. Small, it most certainly was, with a nice high-pile rug under our feet, a round table with chairs in the center, and candles perched on every available surface. There were also plenty of crystals in keeping with the theme of the shop, and posters with blown-up tarot cards adorning the walls.

Mrs. Gorina took a seat at the table and invited us to sit down. "Now, please tell me what seems to be the trouble," she said with a smile.

"The thing is..." I hesitated. This was a very strange story, and I suddenly wondered if we should tell it to this strange woman. She might not take it too well.

"We're the Wraith Wranglers," said Jarrett, who never had such qualms. "You may have heard of us. We're quite famous. And in a bit of a pickle at the moment. At a loss, really, on how to proceed. We've taken on an assignment where a ghost is trying to kill our clients. They murdered him twenty years ago, then locked down his soul with a magical amulet, but now that the amulet is gone—presumably stolen by grave robbers—the ghost has returned to haunt them—and us—and has turned into a ghoul!"

"I see," said the woman, not showing any signs of surprise.

"Oh, and before you criticize our clients—this man was a very bad man, who'd done some very bad things, and he certainly deserved to die. In fact they did the world a favor when they bashed his head in and dumped his body in an unmarked grave."

"Jarrett!" I whispered. "You don't have to tell her the whole story!"

"Why not? She needs to have all the facts at her disposal if she's to help us."

I stared at the woman a little trepidatiously. Help us, or turn us in to the cops?

CHAPTER 18

"I see," said the woman. She placed a pair of wire-rimmed spectacles on her nose and gazed at me sternly. "Harry McCabre and Jarrett Zephyr-Thornton. Oh, yes, I have heard about you. The Wraith Wranglers, occasionally helped by Sir Geoffrey Buckley." A dreamy look came into her eyes. "I was a friend of Buckley's, you know. He used to visit me all the time. Now, not so much."

"I can tell him to visit you, if you'd like," I hastened to say.

"Yes, that would be very nice," she said vaguely. "The thing is, when you're dealing with a ghoul, like the one you just told me about, it's imperative to cast him out before he has the opportunity to carry out his nasty little plan—and trust me, he has a nasty little plan all worked out and ready to bring to fruition."

"What's his plan?" I asked, rubbing my arms to quell the goosebumps that had appeared there.

"I can't tell you. Only the ghoul can, obviously. What I can say is that you have to defend yourselves against him if you are to survive this episode. Oh, yes," she added when we gave gasps of shock, "he does intend to murder you—each and every one of you. Not just your clients but their protectors as well."

"And how do we protect ourselves?" asked Jarrett with croaky voice.

"Wait here," she instructed, and got up and moved off a lot more briskly than I would have expected from someone her age. Moments later, she returned with a string of what looked like gold amulets dangling from red strings. She placed them on the table and sorted through them. There were a few dozen, and they looked like good-luck charms. Some of them depicted dragons, others chickens, and still others serpents. "You need to spread these around your apartment," she said, addressing Jarrett.

He stared down at the charms. "Do I have to? They're quite hideous."

Her lips tightened. "They might be hideous but they'll also protect you. Not to the extent that they will eradicate this evil presence from your lives—but they will weaken its power and its hold over you."

"Its hold?" I asked.

"Yes. Haven't you noticed an increased tendency to bicker? That's the ghoul. He wants to break the bond that unites you so he can better destroy you."

Jarrett nodded. "My boyfriend has been behaving rather strangely lately. He's not usually this mean to me, and last night he called me a... a poofter! Can you credit it?"

Evette placed her hand on the amulets. "That's why you need these."

Jarrett eyed them disdainfully. "The color scheme," he muttered. "It will clash with the furniture."

"What do we do to vanquish this ghoul?" I asked anxiously.

"There is a ritual that must be performed," said Evette.

"I'll teach you the exact words that you have to use, but first you have to find something the ghoul wants."

"What he wants?"

"Yes, tell me what he wants—what he really, really wants," Evette said.

"He wants... the girls, I guess," I said. Then it dawned on me. "Or, rather, one girl in particular. He wants Amaryllis."

"You have to form a circle—hold hands—and then you must place Amaryllis in the heart of the circle. Once you've lured the ghoul into the circle, you must say the words. It's the only way to get rid of it."

"But what about Amaryllis? What's going to happen to her?"

"The moment the ghoul enters the circle, she should flee it, but without breaking it. But whatever you do," she added, leaning forward, "don't allow the ghoul to leave the circle. You will never be able to capture him again, and there is no other way to vanquish him."

We left the shop with the instructions and the amulets, both feeling a little dazed. We'd been up against powerful wraiths before, but this felt different. Personal, somehow. Then again, we'd once fought a wraith who'd murdered Darian's real parents, and we'd managed to destroy it, so why would this time be different? Perhaps because this time five other people depended on us for their survival. Five clients, in fact.

"Do you think we'll manage?" I asked.

"Do you think Amaryllis will agree to act as bait is the more pertinent question," said Jarrett.

"I think she will. As long as we're there to make sure that nothing happens to her."

Jarrett held up the amulets. "I hope Mrs. Magic knows what she's talking about."

"I'm sure she does. Otherwise Buckley would never have pointed her out to us."

We both got into the Rolls, and Jarrett drove us back to the hotel. His driving skills were improving by leaps and bounds ever since he'd started taking over the wheel from Deshawn. "You're almost a great driver," I said. I was riding shotgun, the expensive leather crackling pleasantly beneath my bum.

"Thanks," he said somberly. "I need to be a better driver if I'm going to live my life without Deshawn by my side from now on."

"You're not going to be without Deshawn. He'll come around."

"Not if he's suddenly gone straight on me he won't. Next thing he'll tell me his favorite actor is Sylvester Stallone or Arnold Schwarzenegger and his favorite movie *Rocky* or *Predator* or some such nonsense. Oh, God," he exclaimed, his eyes going wide. "What if he starts listening to rock music? That energy is simply too heavy for me. I won't be able to take it."

I rolled my eyes and stared out the windshield. We had more important things to deal with right now than the heavy energy of rock music. In fact this was probably the toughest assignment we'd had so far, bar none. And if Jarrett was going to fall apart on me, it was going to be that much harder still. "Pull yourself together, Jarrett. I need you."

He glanced over, a hesitant smile on his lips. "You need me? That's the nicest thing you've ever said to me, darling. Maybe I should go straight, too?"

"I'm already spoken for, Jarrett," I reminded him.

"Still. I could go for you. You're pretty. You're sweet. And you give me the space I need. We could be a couple, darling. We could…" He gagged. "We could have sex."

"Oh, for crying out loud. Is the prospect of having sex with me so revolting?"

He grimaced. "It's the boobs, darling. I really don't know what to do with them."

"Well, lucky for you I have a very modest set," I said.

He sighed. "And to be honest, I wouldn't know what to do with the rest of your… equipment."

"It's called a vagina, Jarrett."

He gagged again. "Please. I'm feeling very vulnerable right now."

"Unbelievable," I muttered. "Besides, what makes you think I'd want to have sex with you? You're totally not my type."

He sat up, cut to the quick. "Not your type? I'm everybody's type, darling. I'm handsome, I'm charming, I floss, I'm rich. What's not to like?"

"I guess I like my men tall, dark and mysterious."

"Oh, the myth of the tall, dark stranger, eh? Are you really going there?"

"I am, and for your information, Darian ticks all my boxes."

"Well, I'd tick your box if you'd let me."

"Unless my box makes you throw up, you mean."

He quickly gave me a once-over. "I'm sure I could manage. I'd simply consider it a science experiment. Go in there with an open mind and cleanly washed… utensils."

"You make it sound so romantic, Jarrett. A girl cannot help but swoon."

"I don't want you to swoon. I want you to be knocked off your feet—which you will be, as I would bring my A game and my not inconsiderable stamina."

"Stamina and utensils. I can't wait."

"Of course you can't," he said with a smirk. "They don't

call me Jarrett the ferret for nothing." Then, when he realized what he'd said, he quickly clamped his mouth shut.

I laughed. "Jarrett the ferret? Why?"

He blushed, the first time I'd ever witnessed that phenomenon. "Because."

"Because what?"

He groaned. "Oh, because ferrets can reach tight, dark places in no time without much effort on their part. They get in there and they get the job done. Plus, they're cute and cuddly. Are you happy now? I'm baring my soul here and all you can do is mock me."

"Your ferrety soul," I said. "You know what, Jarrett? Perhaps we should simply stay friends... without benefits."

"Perhaps you're right," he agreed.

We shared a look, and both laughed.

"I love you, darling," said Jarrett.

"And I love you, babe," I said. "Most of the time."

CHAPTER 19

When we arrived home, we found the inhabitants all atwitter. Apparently Courtney had eaten something which had caused her to be sick.

"But what did you have?" asked Jarrett, his hair on end from anxiety.

Courtney, pale as a sheet, pointed to Deshawn. "Shrimp. Something Deshawn whipped up."

We both looked at Deshawn, who was the picture of innocence. "It can't be my sauce. I only used the best ingredients. Perhaps the shrimp were past their expiration date? It's the only thing I didn't check."

"I bought those shrimp myself yesterday morning," said Grace, who stood with her arms folded across her impressive chest. "And they were perfectly fine. In fact I bought some for myself and prepared them last night for dinner."

"Well, I don't know what to tell you," said Deshawn. "Must be one of those allergies."

"I've never been allergic to shrimp before," said Courtney, coughing and looking miserable. "I love shrimp. I eat it all the time."

I regarded Deshawn curiously. Jarrett was right. He did look different. That kindly look that was one of his best features was gone, replaced by a cold, hard stare. Maybe Jarrett was right. Hobnobbing with celebrities and being on TV had changed the man.

"Perhaps we should call a doctor," said Amaryllis, who sat holding Courtney's hand.

But Courtney waved her suggestion away. "I'm fine. I've got nothing left in my stomach so whatever it was, it's gone now. Besides," she added with a brave smile. "We have a show to do, and you can't do a Piquant Pack show without Piquant Pink, can you?"

"No, we certainly can't," said Janell. She clapped her hands. "Let's get going, pack. We need to get there in time if we're going to do this."

In the absence of an actual manager, Janell had taken on the role.

I would have liked to explain to the girls about our visit to Evette, but before I could, they were already rushing out the door, rolling their suitcases with their costumes behind them. The show was a small one, like the one last night, but no less important. There was going to be a lot of press, and the coverage would go a long way to boosting their comeback.

Jarrett had offered the use of his Rolls, so we were traveling in style. And since Deshawn was driving, we were in good hands. Or at least that's what I thought. We hadn't gone three blocks when suddenly Deshawn aimed the Rolls straight for a concrete roadblock the police had set up at a roadwork. If I hadn't jerked his wheel sideways, we would have hit it.

"Oops, my bad," said Deshawn softly, and then he actually smiled!

"What's going on with you?" I cried. "First you almost

poison Courtney and now you almost get us killed? This Bake Off is not having a good effect on you, Deshawn."

"I'm sorry," he said demurely. "I guess my head is not in the right place."

"Well, then get it to the right place. We can't afford any more accidents like this."

"You're right, Harry," he said. "It won't happen again."

I shook my head. As if we didn't have enough on our plate already.

We arrived at the Music Mill with plenty of time to spare. The concert hall was on the outskirts of town, located in an industrial area, and had previously been a factory. It still had an industrial feel to it, and from the outside looked exactly like a nineteenth-century mill, with its saw-tooth roof, its towering red-brick chimney, and its slightly depressing feel. You could sense that once upon a time thousands of workers had slaved away inside the place, checking out their souls at the door the moment they stepped out of the sunlight and onto the gloomy factory floor.

Now, however, the Piquant Pack were going to light the place up with their happy music and their bubbly personalities. I couldn't wait to see them in their element. Since last night's show, I'd been Googling them, and watching old concert footage and videos on YouTube, and I had to admit I recognized a lot of their songs, stuff I had no idea had actually been them. They were really pretty great, and their voices harmonized wonderfully.

People were already lining up outside the entrance when we arrived, and when they saw the Rolls, necks craned and faces lit up expectantly. So when Courtney cracked down the window and waved at the crowd, cheers rang out.

"Looks like we've still got it," Courtney said happily.

"Of course we still got it," said Carrie. "We are the Piquant Pack."

GHOST OF GIRLBAND PAST

Now cheers rang out inside the car as well, and I shared a smile with Jarrett. The girls were hyped up and ready to put on a great show. We drove around the back to where management used to have its offices, and Deshawn parked the Rolls next to a large truck, which had hauled in the material for the concert. And as I got out of the car, I crossed my fingers and hoped that this time everything stayed rigged up and fastened down.

The five ladies were a lively bunch as they got dressed and made up by an eager staff. A representative from the record company was there to discuss some last-minute details about the record launch, and a camera crew from Channel 4 was there to shoot some interviews with the girls. All in all, the atmosphere was electric, and I enjoyed it.

"Maybe we should start a band," I told Jarrett as we lounged on a bright pink couch.

"Maybe we should," he agreed. "Jarrett and the Gang."

"What about me?" I asked. "Why can't I be in the name?"

"There's nothing particularly interesting about Harry, Harry."

"There's plenty interesting about Harry. What about Harry Potter? Prince Harry? Harry Styles? Harry is cool. Loads of people love Harry."

"Yes, but nobody associates the name Harry with singing, Harry."

"Harry Styles!"

"Singing, Harry," he repeated with a grin. "No, I'm just kidding," he said when I punched him lightly on the shoulder. "I love Harry Styles. And I think his singing has improved since his *One Direction* days. And you've got to love those curls."

Deshawn had joined us. He was nervous about the Rolls, I think, because he kept pacing the floor and going out to check if it was still there.

"Relax, Deshawn," I said, clapping him on the back. "Nobody is going to nick the Rolls. There's guards everywhere, and even the police have turned out en masse."

"Yes, they'd have to be crazy to try a stunt," Jarrett agreed. "This is probably the safest place in England right now."

After the accident last night, security had been tightened, and the concert promoter was obviously not taking any chances. The stage had been checked and rechecked and had been declared absolutely safe. Nothing could go wrong. And for the first time I was actually starting to relax. We had been given a method to get rid of the ghost of Aldo Brookfield, and as soon as the concert was over, we were going to explain everything to the girls and ask their cooperation. This was going to work.

The stage manager dropped by to warn the girls that the concert was about to start, and we could hear the music pick up as well as the roar of hundreds of throats clamoring for their favorite band.

The five women stood in a circle. They were dressed in short dresses, each owning their color scheme, and looked fantastic. They now stuck their heads together, then threw up their hands and cried, "Piquant Pack Power!"

I was feeling jazzed up as I walked behind the five women, Jarrett and Deshawn right behind me. And as we walked out onto the stage area, I saw that Buckley was also there. He gave me a wink, which I returned enthusiastically. With Buckley here, nothing could go wrong. He would be able to detect when Aldo was about to strike, and warn us.

We stayed in the wings, and watched as the five superstars walked out in front of the audience, and soon the concert was in full swing.

"They're so great!" I gushed.

"Told you," said Jarrett. "They're the best."

I could sense that his mood was improving as well, which

was a good thing. He and Deshawn even held hands as they sang along with *Hungry*.

"I'm hungry for you," Jarrett squealed, gazing into Deshawn's eyes. *"Doo-bi-doo-bi-doo!"*

"And I'm hungry for you!" Deshawn crooned back. *"Doo-bi-doo-bi-doo!"*

Ah, love. Wasn't it beautiful. And suddenly I wished Darian was here, to share this precious moment with me. I could sing doo-bi-doo-bi-doo to him and he could... And then I saw that Darian *was* here, but when he saw me, he did not look happy.

He'd stepped into the wings on the other side of the stage, a dark look on his face.

"Hey, Darian," I yelled, waving at him.

He caught my eye, but then looked away again. And that's when I saw that he wasn't alone. There were at least a dozen cops with him, and they looked ready for business. What was going on? And as the smile left my face, I saw Darian walk out onto the stage, flanked by his troops, and approach Courtney. Then, in front of the entire concert hall audience, he slapped a pair of handcuffs on her and arrested her!

"Doo-bi-doo-bi-doo," said Jarrett, then frowned. "What's going on? Why is Darian arresting Piquant Pink?"

"Beats me," I said, as I watched Courtney being led off the stage. The hall erupted in loud booing, and the other members of the squad came tripping in our direction. Once they'd reached us, I asked, "What's going on?"

"Courtney was arrested," said Carrie, quite unnecessarily.

"I saw that. But why?"

"For the murder of Aldo!" cried Amaryllis. "Can you believe it?"

"But why?" I realized I was sounding like a broken record, but I didn't get it.

"They found the murder weapon," said Janell. "And it has Courtney's fingerprints all over it."

CHAPTER 20

This was not how Darian had imagined his day would go. He'd hoped to find a moment of quiet time so he could buy Harry some flowers. He'd then show up on her doorstep, hand her the flowers, and take her out for a nice, quiet dinner—just the two of them—where they could talk. He'd wanted to tell her about Isabelle for a long time, but felt uncomfortable dragging up his past in front of her. It wasn't as if he was still pining for Isabelle. After all these years, the pain had dulled, and ever since he met Harry, had almost disappeared entirely, which was a minor miracle.

But then this anonymous phone call had come in, revealing the location of the murder weapon in the Aldo Brookfield murder case. A team of officers had gone down to the time capsule buried on the front lawn of the Cardinal Yardley School and had found the baseball bat that had ended the life of the notorious manager. It had been buried right next to the time capsule, and Aldo Brookfield's body had apparently been buried right on top of it by the looks of things.

When Yardley School management had discovered the

site of the time capsule vandalized, they'd quickly restored it to its former glory, so when Scotland Yard had dug it all up again, they were not very well pleased. All in all they felt that the site had been desecrated to the extent that they'd decided to dig up the time capsule and rebury it in a different location, this time underneath the stone steps leading to the school church.

Hopefully there it would be safe from vandals until the year 2067.

The baseball bat, after thorough examination, had revealed two things: that the blood on it was Aldo Brookfield's. And that the fingerprints were Brookfield's as well, apart from a set that turned out to belong to Courtney Coppola. They had her prints on file from a minor charge brought against her when she was sixteen, and had been arrested for shoplifting along with two of her girlfriends at the time.

"So, Miss Coppola," he said as he sat down across from Courtney in the interview room at Scotland Yard headquarters. "It appears you did not wipe that baseball bat you used to bash your manager's head in." His voice was reproachful, indicating that if you're going to kill a man, the least you can do is wipe your prints from the murder weapon.

"Of course my prints are on that bat," said Courtney disdainfully as she threw the picture of the bat in Darian's face. "I bought that bat."

"You bought that bat," he said skeptically.

"Christmas Eve of the year of our Lord 1994. Back when we got started. Aldo Brookfield was this weaselly bloke who claimed he could take us to the top. I didn't believe him, of course, but when he managed to land us our first number one hit, I bought this bat for him as a thank-you present. I still liked him then—we all did. Little did we know that Aldo would prove to be a horrible little perv I'd rather see dead than alive."

Darian shuffled nervously in his chair. He tried to signal Courtney not to be so outspoken about her wish to see Aldo dead but she ignored him. "So, Miss Coppola, how do you explain this bat turning up at Cardinal Yardley School's time capsule next to the body of your former manager?"

"The murderer must have dumped it in there when he tried to dispose of the body."

"And you're quite sure that that murderer isn't you?"

"Quite sure," she said with an eyeroll. "Look, I told you, I gave the man that baseball bat. Of course it would have my fingerprints on it."

"Is there anyone who can corroborate that story?"

"I have the receipt, if that's what you mean. And there's plenty of pictures of that Christmas party. We were all sozzled to our eyeballs but I do remember Amaryllis was snapping an awful lot of pictures that night. It was our first big break, and we were all excited to finally have liftoff. I think I even ended up snogging with Aldo, at least that's what the pictures say. Personally I don't remember a thing about that night, which is for the best, for the memory of kissing that filthy little toad would keep me up at night."

"Right," he said quickly, wishing she would just stop badmouthing Aldo. "And where can I find those pictures?"

She frowned. "Can I have my phone?"

He signaled to Inspector Fret, who stood guard at the door, making sure Courtney didn't try to escape. The red-haired woman nodded and disappeared for a moment, then returned with Courtney's phone and handed it to the Piquant Pack singer. "Here you go, love."

"Thanks," muttered Courtney, and started flipping through her picture collection. Then she plunked the phone down in front of Darian and tapped it with a long, pink nail. "There you go, guv. Knock yourself out."

He flicked through the pictures, which depicted the five famous members of the girl band in a state of intoxication, imbibing champagne as if it was water, obviously having a whale of a time. At the center of the revels was a red-faced Aldo Brookfield, kissing all the girls and allowing his hands to do all the groping he could manage. It was a little sickening, really.

"Yeah, he was a real peach," said Courtney when she noticed his disapproving frown. "Too bad it took us three years to find out who we were really dealing with."

After going through a batch of the pictures, he finally found one featuring the baseball bat in question. It was as Courtney had told him: the baseball bat, festively wrapped with a pink ribbon, was a gift from her to the manager. They'd even posed for a few shots together, Aldo pretending he was hitting a home run, all the girls cheering loudly. He smiled. "Looks like your story holds up, Miss Coppola."

"Of course it does. And if that's not enough, I can produce the receipt as well." She gave him a knowing look. "I kept it all these years, just in case."

He was afraid to ask what this case might be, so he decided to terminate the interview while he was ahead, and Courtney hadn't told him something she shouldn't. So it was with a wide smile that he got up and held out his hand. "It appears this was all a big misunderstanding, Miss Coppola."

"Courtney," she said with a half-smile as she shook his hand. "How did you find that bat anyway?"

"Anonymous phone call," he said.

"Any idea who called? Might have been the killer."

His smile widened. "Thank you for the tip. We'll certainly take it into consideration."

"No, I'm serious," she said. "You need to look into this

phone call." She held onto his hand as she gave him a look of significance. "It might lead you to a break in the case."

A breakdown, more likely, he thought. He *had* looked into the phone call. Oddly enough, the voice had sounded strangely familiar, as if he'd heard it before. Now that he came to think of it, it had sounded a lot like… Deshawn. Which was impossible, of course. Deshawn was a member of the Wraith Wranglers, and would never willingly try to frame a client for murder.

"Thank you so much for coming in," he said perfunctorily.

"You brought me in, remember?" asked Courtney, a dangerous undertone in her voice. "You arrested me in the middle of our concert, in front of an audience of hundreds of people."

"Yes, I'm sorry about that," he said. "Couldn't be helped, I'm afraid."

She leaned in, still holding onto his hand. "It makes me wonder whose side you're on, Watley."

Well aware that this entire interview was being recorded, and that Commissioner Slack was watching through the one-way mirror, he grinned nervously. "I'm on the side of the victim, of course. As always. Are you a victim, Courtney?"

"Yes, I am," she said. "And I hope for your sake that you recognize that fact."

It had sounded an awful lot like a warning, and uttering threats to a police inspector, especially one investigating the murder of your manager, was not the most clever thing to do. Alas, he was not at liberty to point this out to the irascible singer. Instead, he said, "Please remain available to the investigation. In other words, don't leave town."

She fixed him with a long stare, then nodded and walked out.

Once Courtney was gone, he gathered up his documents and left the interrogation room. Commissioner Slack, a large man with a florid face and a mop of wavy blond hair, took him aside. "So she's cleared or what?"

"Yes, she is, sir. It appears her story holds water."

"Well, I hope you're right," grumbled the Commissioner. "We need to solve this case, Watley, and right speedily, too. Can't have managers whacked all over the place."

He wanted to point out that it was just the one manager that had been whacked, but decided not to voice this retort. He and Commissioner Slack had never seen eye to eye, and ever since Darian had been instrumental in having the Commissioner's son reassigned to the Traffic Unit, their relationship had only worsened.

"Cardinal Yardley School is my alma mater, you see," said the Commissioner. "And I'm not happy about bodies being stuffed all across campus. Sets a bad example."

"Yes, sir," he said resignedly.

"Imagine they'd opened that time capsule in 2067 in front of King William and Queen Catherine and found that bloody corpse inside. It would have been a scandal of epic proportion! An absolute nuisance!"

"I'm sure they would have checked the site before exhuming the capsule, sir."

Commissioner Slack snorted wildly. "Don't be a ruddy fool, man. King William would have put the first spade in the ground, followed by the Queen Consort, and then, before their very eyes, workers would have done the rest. That body would have been found, and the King and Queen would have been there to watch, along with the nation's press hounds, all very eager to snap pictures. Can you imagine the front page of *The Sun*?!"

"If there still is a *Sun* in 2067, sir," he said, which he hoped there wouldn't be.

"Of course there will be a *Sun* in 2067! You can't kill a cockroach, no matter how much you stomp on it. Those festering pests will survive to write about the end of Britain! No, mark my words, Watley. If you don't solve this murder, I will..." He wagged a finger in his face, then made a fist, his face contorted in a scowl, as if yearning to twist Darian's neck personally. "Well, I don't know what I'll do but I can promise you it will be painful. Very, very painful," he said, managing to cover Darian's face in spittle.

As soon as the Commissioner had stalked off, he wiped his face. Solving this murder would be a little tricky, he knew, as he couldn't arrest the real killers, and he could hardly go out and find a patsy to take the fall instead. He uttered a sigh of annoyance. He was exceedingly fond of Harry, but she kept putting him in very awkward positions.

"Darian?" asked Inspector Fret.

"Yes, Tilda?" he muttered as he fingered his chin.

"I'm sure that Aldo Brookfield was killed by a vagrant, sir."

"You are, are you?"

"Yes, sir," she said with a conspiratorial smile. "A vagrant who got into a fight with the notoriously tight-fisted manager, killed him in a fit of rage, buried the body, and then managed to expire himself by getting sauced to the gills, dropping into the River Thames and drowning, sir."

He raised his eyebrows. "And do you have such a vagrant in mind, Tilda?"

"Yes, I do, sir," said the loyal inspector, and produced a file folder.

He perused the file. "Jamil Dove," he muttered. "Known for his volcanic temper. Bar fights. Public intoxication. Aggressive solicitation. Body found June 1997. Cause of death: drowning." He looked up at Tilda. "Sounds like a fine suspect, Inspector."

"Thank you, sir. I've looked into the matter quite deeply, sir."

"Excellent work, Tilda," he said with a smile. "I think you just may have cracked this case."

"Thank you, sir," she said, her freckled face lighting up. "Oh, and sir. What will happen to the Piquant Pack now, sir?" She dropped her voice to a whisper. "You see, I'm a big fan of the girls, sir. A very, very big fan." And she gave him a knowing wink.

Tilda was smart, all right. She'd probably guessed the five women had killed their manager, and was eager to get them off the hook. Under normal circumstances he would have had to reprimand her. Now, he was glad to have her on his team. "Well, now that we have finally caught our killer, all suspicion will be lifted."

She beamed. "Thank you, sir. They deserve to go free. I mean," she quickly added, "they deserve to know who killed their beloved manager."

"Quite so, Tilda," he said. "Quite so."

CHAPTER 21

We met up with Courtney in the police headquarters waiting room. The concert had been canceled and we'd sent the other girls home. They wanted to come, but that hardly seemed feasible as they were very recognizable celebrities and couldn't go anywhere without being hounded for selfies and autographs. And when you're waiting to find out if your friend has been arrested for murder, posing for selfies is the last thing on your mind.

So it was just Jarrett, Deshawn and I who rose to our feet when Courtney finally emerged from the bowels of New Scotland Yard HQ. And judging from the cheeky smile on her lips and the spring in her step she was not going to be remanded in custody just yet.

"What happened?" I asked the moment I saw her.

"Nothing. They found my fingerprints on the murder weapon and figured I put them there when I bashed Aldo's brains in. Good thing I came prepared."

"You did?" I asked, surprised.

"Yup. I've had twenty years to get ready for this, honey. I bought Aldo that bat as a Christmas present, so of course it would have my prints on it. I showed your boyfriend the pictures as proof, offered to hand over the receipt I kept, and that was that. Free to go."

"Phew," said Jarrett. "That was a close call."

"Yes, a very close call," muttered Deshawn, and for some reason he sounded peeved.

I turned to him. "Aren't you happy that Courtney gets to walk free?"

"Of course I am," he said, managing to produce a smile. And as if to prove he wasn't lying, he walked up to Courtney and gave her a hearty hug. A very hearty hug, actually, as I watched his hands wander to her butt.

"Hey there, slugger," said Courtney with a laugh. "Off limits to bakers."

"I'm sorry," said Deshawn with a tight smile. "I guess I got carried away by my sheer joy of watching you escape a murder charge. It's so gratifying to see justice done."

"Yes," said Courtney happily. "Looks like we're finally off the hook."

"Yes, looks like," said Deshawn, his smile morphing into a scowl. "So can I take you home now, my lady?"

"I think I will take you up on that offer, Deshawn."

"Your carriage awaits," he said while bobbing a slight curtsy.

"You guys go on home," I said. "I want to talk to Darian first."

"You do that," said Jarrett, directing a scathing look at Deshawn, probably in reference to the butt-grabbing incident. "And tell him to stop sabotaging our clients' comeback tour."

"He's only doing his job, Jarrett," I reminded him.

"Yes, well, he should wait until after the tour is done."

I smiled as I approached the desk. Try telling the police to wait to investigate a murder until after the suspects have finished touring the country. I asked the constable womanning the desk if she could tell Inspector Watley that he had a visitor, and she immediately relayed the message. I could have called Darian, but I knew I would have to sign the visitor's log anyway, so official channels seemed like the best way to go.

Five minutes later, Darian arrived and we decided to go for a walk.

"The walls have ears in there," he said as we passed the pool with the eternal flame and walked down the few steps to the sidewalk. "And we don't want everyone to know I just released a suspect, knowing full well she's guilty of the charges."

"This must be hard for you," I intimated.

"Yes, it is," he said, drawing his fingers through his dark hair. As usual, he looked stunningly handsome with his classic features and well-cut suit, though judging from the shadows beneath his eyes, this investigation wasn't going the way he'd hoped.

"So is Courtney off the hook now?"

"Yes—yes, I think that's a reasonable assumption. Though to be on the safe side, I need to produce a credible suspect to replace her. And Tilda seems to have found one."

"You found... a fake killer?"

"I can't believe I'm saying this but yes, it appears that I have." He raised a finger. "And please don't tell my dad, for he's going to kill me if he ever finds out what I did." He handed me his phone and I found myself staring at the mug shot of a disheveled-looking man who looked as drunk as a fiddler. "I present to you Mr. Dove. Now our best suspect in the murder of Aldo Brookfield."

"Isn't Mr. Dove going to have something to say about that?"

"Jamil Dove won't have anything to say. Jamil Dove has

been dead for twenty years. But very conveniently for us, he only died after he bashed Brookfield's head in."

"He did, did he?"

"If he didn't before, he most certainly did now." He heaved a deep sigh. "How low I've sunk. And to think I've only got myself to thank for this—and you, of course."

"Me! How is this my fault?"

He gave me a grim smile. "Honey, do you honestly believe I'd do this for everyone? If you hadn't convinced me to cover for the Piquant Five, I wouldn't be doing this."

"The Piquant Pack," I said. "They're not the Famous Five, Darian."

"Well, there are five of them, and they are famous," he argued.

"Look, I appreciate what you're doing," I said. "I really do, but don't blame it on me. You made a choice that night at the graveyard."

He arched an eyebrow. "You mean the Cardinal Yardley Roman Catholic School?"

I smiled. "Exactly."

"Did you know that school is Commissioner Slack's alma mater?"

"Why am I not surprised?"

"He wasn't pleased that King William and Queen Catherine would be digging up Aldo's corpse in 2067. Not pleased at all."

I laughed. "That would have been something."

"At least if the monarchy survives until then."

"I'm pretty sure it will. And so will the music of the Piquant Pack. At least if they manage to stay out of prison long enough to finish this tour."

He patted his phone. "Jamil Dove will make sure of that."

"Give him my regards."

"I'll give your regards to Tilda. This was her idea. She's a big Piquant Pack fan."

"You mean Tilda guessed that the girls did this?"

Darian nodded. "I guess she did."

"That's worrisome. What if more colleagues of yours guessed the same thing?"

"I don't think so, Harry. Tilda is one of the brightest inspectors I know, and very observant, which is not something that can be said about all of them. I'm sure our secret is safe."

I placed a hand on his arm. "Thanks, Darian. I know you went above and beyond the call of duty. Not to mention this could have cost you your career."

"You can thank me tonight," he said. "Over a nice dinner for two."

"I'm afraid dinner is off for the time being. Until we manage to exorcise this ghoul, I'm not leaving the girls' side for one second." And I proceeded to tell him about the visit Jarrett and I had paid to Evette Gorina, and the ritual she'd suggested.

"This all sounds very dangerous, Harry," said Darian with a worried frown. "Are you sure you can trust this woman?"

"Buckley recommended her, so yes, I trust her."

He halted in mid-stride. "Promise me you'll be careful."

"I will. Nothing will happen to me, Darian. I have my own guardian angel."

"You do," he said, "but even I can't protect you all the time."

I'd actually been thinking about Buckley, but Darian was right. He was as much my guardian angel as Buckley was. "I'll be fine," I said reassuringly. "I mean, what can go wrong, right?"

Talk about famous last words…

CHAPTER 22

We were all seated in the living room of Jarrett's suite, and when I glanced around, I was greeted with looks of determination on the girls' faces.

"Yes," said Janell. "We'll do this. Won't we, girls?"

"So… we just sit in a circle and hold hands and that's how we'll get rid of Aldo?" asked Amaryllis. She gave me a look of uncertainty. "Are you sure that's going to work?"

"Yes, it will," I said, trying to sound more confident than I was feeling. Frankly, both Jarrett and I were way out of our depth here, and I just hoped Evette wasn't a kook.

Jarrett, carefully placing the last of the amulets on top of a portrait of himself and Deshawn, eyed it disdainfully. He'd been vocally opposed to ruining his suite's esthetics with these hideous amulets, and now that the entire place was festooned with them, his annoyance had only increased.

"What are those for?" asked Carrie. "Those funny-looking charms?"

"They're for protection," I said. "To weaken Aldo's power."

At that moment, Deshawn walked in, carrying a tray laden with cups of tea, cucumber sandwiches and ginger biscuits. "Oh, did you make these yourself?" asked Courtney excitedly.

"Yes, I did," Deshawn announced, setting down the tray on the end table.

For a moment, I caught him glancing at the amulets, and the look in his eye told me he felt exactly the same way about them as Jarrett did: he disliked them thoroughly.

"They're only for the time being," I told him. "As soon as we get rid of Aldo's ghost we'll remove them again."

"Of course," he said, but couldn't hide his displeasure.

"So when are we doing this?" asked Carrie.

"What about right now?" I suggested. "The sooner we get this over with, the better."

"Oh, but don't we need to prepare the room?" asked Amaryllis. "Like put garlic everywhere and crucifixes and maybe cook up some kind of special herbal brew?"

"We're trying to get rid of a ghost, Amaryllis," said Janell. "Not a vampire."

The blond-haired singer giggled. "Oh, my. I guess I got my exorcisms all screwed up, haven't I?"

So without further ado, we all took a seat on Jarrett's white carpet, formed a circle, and held hands, closing the circle. And now for the hard part.... "Amaryllis?" I asked. "Will you please take a seat inside the circle?"

"Me?" she asked with wide-eyed surprise. "But I like it here."

"You're going to act as bait," said Janell. "Isn't that right, Harry?"

"That's exactly right," I said. "Aldo seems to have a crush on you, so if you sit down in the middle of the circle, it should draw him out and make him join you."

"But I don't want him to join me! I don't want that creep anywhere near me!"

At this, Deshawn uttered a low growl, and the scowl on

his face indicated he wasn't happy about all these delays. He probably had more cakes to bake for the Bake Off. "Just do it already," he grunted, which just went to show how much he'd changed.

"Yes, just do it already, honey," said Janell. "He's not going to harm you."

"How do you know? You're not the one who's acting as live bait!"

"We're right here, remember? We're going to protect you."

"Are you sure?" she asked with a pout.

"We won't let anything happen to you," Carrie said. "Scout's honor."

"You were never in the scouts," said Amaryllis.

"I was, and I promise you that everything will be fine," said Courtney.

Amaryllis nodded. "All right. Fine. But if I get raped and slaughtered I'm coming back to haunt you."

We all laughed nervously, though it really wasn't all that funny.

"It's a good thing you know what you're doing, Harry," said Amaryllis as she crawled in the center of the circle. "And that I trust you completely."

"Thanks," I said, and had to stifle an audible gulp. Know what I was doing? I had no idea what I was doing!

Fortunately for me and my raging nerves, just then Buckley arrived on the scene, taking a seat right next to me. "It'll be fine," he murmured and squeezed my shoulder.

"Right," I said. "Let's do this."

I placed the text I'd received from Evette in front of me on the carpet, took Jarrett's hand in my left, Janell's hand in my right, and started intoning the words, imbibing them with as much meaning as I could.

"Spirit of Aldo Brookfield, we summon you here now. We

summon you into this circle of trust. Join us now, spirit of Aldo Brookfield, and flock to without delay."

It went on like that for a while, and when I'd reached the end of the page, I simply started from the top again. After I'd done this for ten minutes or so, my throat was really dry, and as far as I could see there was no sign of Aldo Brookfield. I did notice that Deshawn was scowling at me, as if he couldn't wait to get out of there. I read on for another ten minutes but by then it was obvious that Aldo was a no-show. Dang it.

"I don't think he'll show up," said Buckley.

"I think you're right," I said with a sigh.

"This Evette woman is quite obviously a fraud," said Deshawn now, getting up and breaking the connection. He stretched. "Just a big bunch of baloney!"

"I don't think she's a fraud," I said pensively. "Something else is going on."

"Maybe Aldo left already?" asked Amaryllis hopefully. She was glad to be let out of the circle and quickly crawled away and plunked herself down onto the couch. "Maybe he's gone and we're just scared of nothing?"

"She's right," said Carrie. "If Aldo was still around, he would have attacked us at the show this afternoon. Instead, that inspector showed up and arrested Courtney."

"After someone placed an anonymous call to reveal the location of the murder weapon," I reminded her. "And who else could have made that call but Aldo himself?"

"Ghosts don't use the phone," said Jarrett. "So that rules out Aldo."

"Who else could it have been?" I asked.

"The kids who stole the amulet, obviously," said Deshawn. "They found the amulet, saw the body and the baseball bat and called it in. Civic duty and all that rot."

I frowned at Deshawn. He was acting so strange... "If it

was those kids they would have called sooner," I argued. "Why wait until now?"

"They had to screw up their courage," said Deshawn. "Had to convince themselves this was the right thing to do. And good thing they did, too."

"Good thing they did?" asked Courtney. "I got arrested thank you very much."

"No, I don't mean that, of course," said Deshawn quickly. "I mean, it's great to know that the future of Britain is in such good hands. Young lads with a moral compass."

He quickly looked away when I studied him closely. "No," I said. "Something tells me that Aldo isn't gone yet. He'll be back."

"Oh, I hope not," said Amaryllis with a shiver. "This is all too awful."

"It's all right," said Janell, taking a seat next to her and covering her friend's hand with hers. "When he shows up, we'll catch him. We caught him once, we'll do it again. Only this time we'll make sure he never shows his ugly face again." And at this, she directed a grin at Deshawn.

CHAPTER 23

A quiet shiver ran through the apartment as Aldo, still cloaked in the body of Deshawn Little, moved from room to room. He was still incensed at that clown Darian Watley. A man who dared call himself a Scotland Yard inspector had willingly and knowingly colluded with these wretched Wraith Wranglers to pervert the law! It was an outrage! He'd hoped, by calling in the location of that baseball bat, that at least Courtney would be locked in jail for the rest of her miserable life, which only left the four others to deal with. But no, that inspector just had to be Harry's boyfriend.

He stared down at Amaryllis, a leering expression on his face. A thought had occurred to him earlier. Now that he had a body again, he might as well make good use of it and ravage that pretty blond bimbo the way she should be ravished. Only problem was, her screams would alert the others quicker than he could say, "Hello, poppet."

He licked his lips—or rather that fat butler's lips. He should have picked that moron Jarrett's body. With a body like that, a man could do some real damage. Deshawn's? Not exactly. The man had a keen sense of hygiene, though, he had to give him that. He'd never known a man so crazy about manscaping as this stupid sod. Top to bottom not a single hair on his body! Amazing. And weird. And then there was this crazy tattoo on the guy's left butt cheek. It looked like an Indian, but it could also be a shaman. Or possibly some old lover. It was just his luck to end up inside the body of a poof! Karma worked in mysterious ways, that was for sure.

He took out the knife he'd picked up in the kitchen. It was one of those big butcher knives and would serve his purpose just fine. All he had to do now was make sure that they kept their tongues when he slit their throats, so they wouldn't alert the others. He'd do the five women first, then this annoying Harry McCabre, and then finally Jarrett. Then he'd sneak out and start a new life, living in the body of this funny-looking queer.

And he raised the knife, eager to slash Amaryllis's throat in one thrust, when suddenly he experienced a strange weakening sensation in his arm. And as he brought it down, his fingers lost their grip on the knife and it fell from his grasp.

With a frown, he picked it up again, but then felt his entire body go limp, incapable of summoning up the strength to stay erect, much less murder Piquant Blond.

What the hell was going on? Was Deshawn's body malfunctioning on him? Was he having a seizure or something? But he had seemed so unnaturally healthy and fit!

And that's when he saw it: the amulet. Draped across the headboard of the bed. He tried to reach it, but felt himself deflating like the national budget, his energy draining away. It was all he could do to snatch the knife and crawl from the room on hands and knees. And only when he'd put some distance between himself and the amulet, did he feel his strength return. He shook his fist in rage. For he knew that that moronic fathead Jarrett had placed amulets in all the bedrooms, not to mention every other place in this stupid suite.

"Deshawn? Is that you?" asked a voice from the darkness. He recognized it as Harry's. The fathead's little idiot friend.

"Yes, it's me," he managed. "I just wanted to check if everything was all right."

The light was switched on and he quickly kicked the knife underneath the sofa.

"And? Are they okay?"

"Yes. Nothing to worry about, Harry," he said, spiriting a fake smile onto his face and getting up. "I thought I saw something on the floor," he explained. "But it's fine."

"What do you think about this whole thing?" asked Harry. "Do you believe Aldo is gone?"

"Oh, yes," he said. "I'm sure he felt the Wraith Wranglers were no match for him and he decided to skip out early."

She wrinkled her nose. "I don't think so, actually. I have a strong suspicion he's still around."

"But then why hasn't he shown his face?" he argued.

"I don't know," she admitted. "But I asked Buckley before? And he said he still senses him. He just can't put his finger on it. It's almost as if…"

"As if what?" he asked with a pang of worry. He hoped that old fruitcake hadn't spotted him.

"As if he's hiding in plain sight. Those were Buckley's words."

He laughed. "Where could he be hiding? There's no place to hide from Buckley. Right?" he asked nervously.

"Normally there isn't. Buckley should be able to spot another ghost quite easily. Only he hasn't, and it's got me worried."

"Maybe your Buckley is losing his touch. That's also a possibility to consider."

"Our Buckley," she was quick to correct him. "And are you suggesting Buckley is senile?"

"Ha ha," he laughed. "Of course not. Buckley still has all his marbles. Sharp as a tack, that man."

"He is," she said with a smile. "Well, I'm glad you think Aldo's gone. And maybe you're right. Maybe he did feel outnumbered and outgunned. We'll know soon enough."

"Why's that?"

"Tomorrow is a big day for the Piquant Pack. Perhaps the biggest day of their lives. They're getting their OBEs from the hands of the Queen herself. If Aldo wanted to hit them where it hurts the most, he would strike when the ceremony is in full swing, the eyes of the whole nation on them."

"Right," he said slowly, a malevolent gleam in his eyes as he rubbed his hands.

"Good night, Deshawn. Try not to wake Jarrett when you turn in. You know how miffed he gets when he doesn't get his Zs." And at this, she switched off the light.

Aldo stealthily moved back to the bedroom he shared with Jarrett, and as he crawled beneath the sheets, he knew exactly what he had to do. And as he turned his back on Jarrett, he grinned evilly. His smile soon disappeared, however, as Jarrett hugged him from behind, and muttered sleepily, "Let's spoon, darling. Yesss. That's it. That's the spot…"

CHAPTER 24

I was honored to be invited to join the Piquant Pack as guests when they became Officers of the Most Excellent Order of the British Empire. I'd met Her Royal Highness the Queen once, and had even spent some time chatting with her and her husband in her bedroom. At the time, we were all under attack, and had had a narrow escape. I didn't think she'd remember, though, as she probably met so many people throughout the day—or night.

We were seated in the Ballroom, a large and ornately furnished room in Buckingham Palace, the carpet a vivid burgundy, as was the chairs' upholstery. Sconces bathed the room in a golden light while white marble columns lent the whole an almost church-like ambiance. Below pristinely white arches, two thrones stood on a dais, where I assumed the Queen would take her place, along with her King Consort. Behind us on the balcony, a band was playing.

When the Queen finally entered, she wasn't accompanied by her husband, however, but by a bunch of funnily-dressed men, and a stiff-looking white-haired gentleman dressed in a blue costume with plenty of insignia pinned to his lapels.

"That's the Lord Chamberlain," said Jarrett, leaning in to whisper in my ear. "He's the one who calls out the names of the recipients so the Queen can do her thing."

"Great fun," I said as I glanced around. Plenty of people were getting their awards today, it appeared. Athletes, businesspeople, artists, organizers of charitable foundations... All had achieved something in life that warranted this rare recognition. They were all waiting in the next room, to be led in when their name came up on the list.

From where we were sitting I could see that the five Piquant Pack members were up next. Once the Queen was in position, Janell was called forward, and she walked up to Her Majesty, eyes bright. Once she reached the Monarch, Her Royal Highness tapped Janell's shoulders with a sword and then pinned a medal of some kind to her dress.

"I love this," I said. "It's all so nice."

Yes, I can't help it. I'm a royalist at heart, I guess, and love all the pomp and circumstance that surrounds the whole thing.

"Don't you love it, Deshawn?" I asked. He'd been very quiet throughout, and had hardly spoken a word since the Queen had arrived. Awestruck to be in the presence of royalty, I assumed.

"Yes," the demure baker said. "Yes, it's very nice."

Nice wasn't exactly the word I'd have used. Impressive, perhaps. Or unique. And I was sitting up, vowing to take it all in and enjoy every second of this experience, when Amaryllis walked in, a smile on her face, and ready to receive her award. And the Queen had just raised her sword to tap her lightly on the shoulder, when Deshawn suddenly got up out of his seat and jogged to the front of the room, grabbed the sword from Her Majesty, and thrust it at Amaryllis with a clear aim to wound, maim or kill!

Marisol Glee, the famous songstress, who'd been next in

line to receive her award, looked nonplussed. "I want an OBE," she muttered.

"Deshawn!" cried Jarrett, on his feet. "Are you mad?!"

Deshawn was still trying to put a hole in Amaryllis, who'd uttered a blood-curdling scream and was running around like a headless chicken, Deshawn in hot pursuit. The funnily-dressed men were all running after Deshawn, while more funnily-dressed men poured into the room and gathered around the Queen, in order to protect her from this maniac.

Deshawn streaked past us, and when I saw the crazed expression on his face, and noticed how he was actually foaming at the mouth, I finally realized what must have happened.

"It's Aldo!" I cried. "He took possession of Deshawn!"

Jarrett, who was busy pulling at his hair, exclaimed "What?!"

"He must have jumped inside his body and taken possession! That's why he's been acting so strange. And why he tried to poison Courtney. Or wreck the Rolls with all of us in it! He's possessed!"

"Deshawn!" squealed Jarrett. "My precious!"

Oh, dear. This wasn't good. If those guys caught Deshawn, there was no telling what they might do. And if Deshawn caught Amaryllis, he'd poke a hole in her!

Amaryllis was quickly losing ground. Even though she was running for her life, it was obvious she was also running out of steam. Deshawn, even though I'd never pegged him for a runner, was gaining on her fast, while the cavalry that was trying to catch him was still far behind. The Queen, meanwhile, watched the proceedings with customary equanimity.

"We have to do something!" I said.

"But what?!" Jarrett retorted.

"This," I said, and stuck out my foot just as Deshawn came

passing by me for the third time. He fell flat on his face, and instantly about a dozen men piled on top of him, just the way you sometimes see on those American football games.

"Oh, my poor Deshawn!" Jarrett cried, plucking some more at his hair.

Meanwhile, the Queen had spotted us, for she narrowed her eyes in my direction. Uh-oh. "I think the Queen remembers us, Jarrett," I said, pointing at the Monarch.

"Oh, no. There goes our royal warrant!"

"She'll probably think we had something to do with this."

"You think? That's Deshawn down there, covered by those brutes!"

Just then, a ghost emerged from the pileup, and I saw it was Aldo Brookfield. "Get back here, you!" he was yelling, and then streaked down in the direction of poor Amaryllis, who was just trying to catch her breath, surrounded by her four friends.

A thunderous sound rumbled, and suddenly the room was plunged into darkness. Then lightning flashed down from the ceiling, and hit the floor right next to the Piquant Pack.

"I'm coming for you," Aldo said with a cruel grin. "This time you won't get away!"

And just as he launched himself at the fivesome, Buckley appeared out of nowhere, and knocked the vicious ghost out of course.

"Hey, you old fruitcake! Watch where you're going!"

"Who are you calling an old fruitcake, you murderous creep?!" boomed Buckley, and slammed into Aldo's ghost again, this time taking him through the window, which exploded into a thousand pieces, eliciting cries of terror from the people in the Ballroom. The Queen's Guard followed the fight between the two ghosts with bated breath, and as Buckley and Aldo battled it out, the big chandelier that hung suspended above us, suddenly exploded and came crashing down. Before it hit us, Buckley suddenly streaked down, and dragged us out of the path of destruction.

Aldo, spotting an opportunity, came barreling down, aiming for Amaryllis. But before he could reach her, Buckley was there once again, and blocked him by delivering the most wonderful right hook I'd ever seen.

The blow was so powerful that Aldo was knocked straight through yet another window, which flew apart on impact, and I think the ghost decided that enough was enough, for we could hear his voice in the distance. "I'll get you for this! This isn't over! I'll be back!"

And then it was over.

Jarrett helped me up, and we both watched as Deshawn was led away by armed guards. The man looked absolutely flabbergasted. "Wha—what's going on?" he asked.

"Don't worry, Deshawn," Jarrett told him as he was led past us. "We'll get you out."

"What happened?" he asked, shaking his head, dazed and confused.

"You were possessed," I said. "Aldo possessed you."

But then he was gone, escorted from the room. When I looked up, I saw that the Queen was standing right next to me. I started violently, as I hadn't heard her approach.

"Harry McCabre," said the Monarch, fixing me with a stern look. "You again."

"Yes, me again, Your Highness," I said. "I'm very sorry about all of this."

"Can you tell them to let Deshawn go, Your Majesty?" asked Jarrett. "He's innocent."

"If you mean by Deshawn the man who just tried to murder that poor woman, no, I most certainly will not let him go, young man. Are you mad?"

"He wasn't himself," I explained.

"No, I should think not."

"No, I mean, he was possessed. By the ghost of the Piquant Pack's dead manager."

The Queen pursed her lips. "The man who's been disturbing their concerts? Oh, yes. I am a fan. In fact I was going to invite them to perform at my birthday party."

"They're being haunted by their old manager," I explained. "And since he was unable to get at them, he decided to jump into the body of Jarrett's boyfriend instead."

"I see," the Queen mused. "That changes matters. So what do you propose I do about this?"

"I'm not sure," I confessed.

She pursed her lips reproachfully. "Harry McCabre is not sure. Well, I guess that means we're all doomed."

"We simply have to repeat last night's ritual," said Jarrett. "It didn't work because Aldo was right there, joining hands with us. Without him, it just might work."

"No, it won't," I argued. "He knows we're trying to trap him. He won't fall for that."

"Well, while you try to work things out, I'll have to have my palace rebuilt, I guess," said the Queen, darting a sad glance at the broken windows.

"And what about Deshawn?" Jarrett asked eagerly.

The Queen raised an imperious eyebrow. "What about him?"

"Are you going to let him go?"

"Honestly, Mr. Zephyr-Thornton. Do you really expect me to persuade the Queen's Guard to release the man who attacked a guest with a sword and then proceeded to single-handedly destroy my entire Ballroom? I don't think so."

"But it wasn't him," said Jarrett desperately. "He was possessed."

She produced a wan smile. "I may be a believer, Mr. Zephyr, but the rest of the nation isn't there yet." After a long pause, she finally nodded. "But I'll see what I can do. As long as you promise me to stay away from Buckingham Palace from now on."

"Yes, Ma'am," Jarrett and I said dutifully.

She walked away, then turned back. "Oh, and catch that horrible manager!"

CHAPTER 25

"We would like to announce that we're quitting," said Janell. The other members of the Piquant Pack stood next to her with bowed heads—except for Courtney, who was facing the pack of media hounds head-on, as if defying them to say something.

We were right outside Buckingham Palace, where the media had gathered to catch a first glimpse of the OBE recipients, as they always did at the end of the investiture. This time, however, they got a lot more than they'd bargained for. First there was the as yet unconfirmed story of a *Great British Bake Off* contestant who'd lost his marbles and had gone after the Queen with a sword, and had managed to demolish a big chunk of the Royal Palace, and now here were the Piquant Pack themselves, announcing they were quitting their comeback tour!

"As you are well aware by now, what was supposed to be the highlight of our lives and careers, the reception of this amazing honor, was marred by an incident. It has made us realize that stepping back into the limelight has caused heartache and pain not only to our own families but other people as well. We cannot condone this kind of violence, and prefer to retreat back into obscurity. We thank all of our fans, and the people who stood by our side as we staged this tour, and hope you will forgive us."

She stepped away from the microphone, ignoring the clamoring press people, peppering her with questions. She turned to me. "I know you don't agree with me, Harry, but it's the only way to stop the violence." She directed an anxious look at Jarrett. "We never meant for Deshawn to get hurt, Jarrett. And I feel terrible about what happened."

"It's not your fault," said Jarrett. "Aldo must have taken Deshawn by surprise. And I'm sure he wouldn't want you to quit over this. He's as big a fan as I am, and he would want you to go on—fight the good fight and finally take Aldo down."

"We can't risk any more lives over this," said Amaryllis, still shaken after the recent events. "Things have gone too far and it's time to call it quits."

"I agree," said Courtney, directing a critical eye at the media circus that was unfolding in front of us. "It isn't worth losing good people like Deshawn over."

"Oh, I do hope he'll be all right," said Perpetua. "He looked so stricken and confused."

"How would you feel if you'd just been possessed by an evil spirit and forced to murder a bunch of people?" asked Carrie. She shook her head. "We should never have announced our comeback. This was all a mistake. A very big mistake."

"No, it wasn't," I said. "How could you possibly have known that Aldo would stage a comeback, too? There was no way you could have foreseen this. You're not responsible, you guys. Aldo is."

"Our decision is final, Harry," said Janell. "We're breaking up the band. Again."

"Oh, no," said Jarrett, who was on the verge of tears. "First Deshawn gets arrested and now you are breaking up the band? This is the worst day of my life!"

"It could have been worse," said Courtney. "Aldo could have skewered Amaryllis."

"Ooh!" cried Amaryllis, her hands flying to her belly to make sure there were no puncture wounds. "Imagine being skewered by the Queen's saber! What a way to go down in history!"

"It would definitely have been headline news," Janell agreed with a comforting smile.

"So what's going to happen to Deshawn?" asked Amaryllis. "Is he going to be in jail long?"

"Well, he did just try to murder a person in front of the Queen," said Courtney. "So I doubt very much if even Darian Watley can make this go away. Too many witnesses, one of whom is the Queen herself."

"Not to mention all those cameras," I said. "Though I wonder what they'll make of the whole light show at the end. That wasn't Deshawn."

"Oh, they will pin it on him," said Jarrett somberly. "Trust the press to do that."

"So what's next?" asked Carrie. "Where do we go from here?"

"Right back to the apartment," I said. "Where you'll be protected by the amulets."

"Do you really think those work?" asked Janell.

"Yes, I do. Why else did Aldo wait to attack until now? He could have killed us in our sleep but he didn't. I think that's because those amulets drained his power to such an extent he couldn't go through with it."

"That's very well possible," Janell agreed.

"So we're going to have to stay at Jarrett's place for the rest of our lives now?" asked Courtney.

"That's impossible," said Perpetua. "The kids are already asking when I'm coming home. And Brad won't like me staying at the Ritz-Carlton indefinitely either."

"I could get used to it," said Carrie. "I like it there. It's definitely better than home."

"Thank you," said Jarrett, who probably wouldn't mind having the Piquant Pack stay at his suite forever.

"We have to find a way to vanquish Aldo permanently," I said. "To make him go away and never come back." I turned to Jarrett. "And we have to pay a visit to Deshawn. He'll be terrified."

We arrived at Scotland Yard headquarters twenty minutes later. A phone call to Darian had told us Deshawn had already been remanded to the custody of Scotland Yard, and would be interrogated about his role in the investiture disaster shortly. Unfortunately, Darian was not in charge, even though he'd tried to establish the link between the death of Aldo Brookfield twenty years ago and this murderous rampage of Deshawn's just now. Commissioner Slack hadn't gone for it, though, claiming these were two totally unrelated events.

We were allowed a short visit with Deshawn, and only after Darian had pulled some strings. After this, the only visitor Deshawn was going to be allowed to entertain was his solicitor.

He looked a little wan, which was hardly surprising. The small room where we sat was guarded by two burly Scotland Yard officers, and a third guard had been placed inside the room, next to the door, and kept darting murderous glances in our direction. We were seated at a table, in bright orange plastic chairs that looked more at home in the seventies.

"How are you holding up, darling?" asked Jarrett solicitously.

"Well, they're treating me well enough, I suppose," said Deshawn. "Though I have to admit it is a far cry from the luxury of the Ritz-Carlton. And I don't like these clothes very much." He gestured at the pajama-like gray outfit he was wearing.

"Yes, they are awful," Jarrett agreed. "At least you're not wearing one of those orange jumpsuits. You know what orange does to your complexion, darling."

"I know. That would have been absolutely terrible."

Jarrett nodded sadly. "I wish there was something I could do, but they're refusing to budge on this one."

"I understand," said Deshawn. "I did try to murder the Queen, right?" He shivered. "How did this happen? I can't understand. I love Her Majesty. Adore her."

"Aldo must have jumped into your body when you weren't looking," said Jarrett.

"Probably while you were asleep," I said.

"I don't remember a single thing," said Deshawn. "Not a single thing. All I remember is waking up on the floor of that Ballroom with a bunch of people sitting on my back."

"And what is the last thing you remember before that?" I asked.

He frowned. "Well, I've been trying to recollect, and the memory that stands out the most is the five members of the Piquant Pack enjoying my baking efforts so much they were all over me."

"I remember," said Jarrett acerbically, his compassion waning.

"Of course now that's all over," said Deshawn, hanging his head disconsolately. "I'm sure they already replaced me on the Bake Off, and it looks like I'll spend the rest of my life locked up in a concrete box somewhere, never to see the light of day again." he sighed deeply. "Or to smell the delicious scent of freshly baked pastry." He directed a sad look at Jarrett. "Or to cuddle up to my snuggly bunny ever again."

"Oh, Deshawn," said Jarrett with a sob. "Our wedding plans."

"All phut."

"I'll wait for you, darling. I'll wait for you forever."

"Oh, no, Jarrett, don't. You can't waste your life. Move on, darling. You'll find love again. And as for me…" He closed his eyes. "Just… forget about me. Forget I ever lived."

"But I can't, darling. I can't forget you."

"Please do. It's for the best."

"Oh, stop all this melodrama," I said. "Can't you hire a decent lawyer, Jarrett? I thought you were the richest man in the country."

"I am," said Jarrett, his face lighting up. "Of course I am. Oh, Deshawn, I'll get you the best lawyer money can buy. I'll get you a dozen lawyers. They'll get you out of here in a jiffy."

Well, maybe not a jiffy. I doubt whether you can crash the Queen's party, steal her sword and chase her guests around with it and get away with it. Still, it was worth a shot. And hadn't Her Majesty promised us she would 'see what she could do?' Perhaps Deshawn had a shot at getting out of here before he was old and gray.

The guard at the door announced in a stentorian voice, "Time's up!"

Jarrett and Deshawn needed a few moments to say goodbye, so I discreetly turned my back on them. There were sounds of smooching.

Finally, the guard growled, "I said time's up, you sorry lot!"

And that's how our visit to Deshawn ended. It was sad to see him like that. The proud former butler-slash-valet looked so forlorn as he shuffled out of the visitors' room, escorted by the three guards.

When we walked out, Darian was waiting for us.

"I'm sorry," he said. "There's nothing I can do. My hands are tied. The Commissioner wants to petition Whitehall to bring back the death penalty. Says Deshawn should be hanged, drawn and quartered for this."

"Did they ever hang, draw and quarter people when capital punishment still existed?" I asked.

"I doubt it, but Slack seems adamant it should be reinstated. Claims Deshawn is probably working for some foreign enemy and he would love nothing more than to take him down to the Tower of London and apply some of those old torture methods on him."

"Oh," Jarrett said, breaking down. "This is all some horrible, horrible nightmare! Tell me I'm going to wake up soon and none of this will have happened, Harry."

"I'm afraid it did happen," I said. "It's still happening, actually."

"They're not going to murder Deshawn," Darian assured Jarrett. "No matter how much Slack wants, he can't have Deshawn chopped up into little pieces."

"Oh!" Jarrett whimpered. "Oh, dear!"

"I think you better dial down on the torture talk, Darian," I said.

"Right," he agreed. "Well, I'll do what I can, of course, which isn't much, I'm afraid." He fixed me with a keen look, and placed his hands on my shoulders. "That could have been you, Harry. Aldo could have picked you to possess and use as a vessel for his evil plans."

"Thank God he didn't," I said with a shiver. "Or I would be the one about to be hanged, drawn and quartered—oh, I'm so sorry, Jarrett. I didn't mean…"

But Jarrett was inconsolable. And as he staggered away

toward the exit, wailing like a banshee, I watched him go with pain in my heart. "Poor sod," said Darian, which was a first for him. He wasn't exactly a big fan of Jarrett's. "I don't think I've ever seen him like this."

"I guess Deshawn really is the love of his life."

We were both silent for a beat, then Darian surprised me by suddenly clasping his arms around me and hugging me close. He proceeded by kissing me no less than a dozen times in quick succession, and then breathed, "I never realized more than today how dangerous this Wraith Wranglers business is, Harry. I don't think I could stand it if anything happened to you."

"Nothing is going to happen to me," I assured him, though I wasn't sure if I believed it myself. After today, it looked like anything was possible. Even the worst-case scenario. "We're going to defeat Aldo, get Deshawn his royal pardon, and watch the Piquant Pack launch the most successful tour in the history of this country."

Darian held me at arm's length for a moment and studied my face. Then he smiled. "You are by far the most optimistic person I've ever met."

"Which is why you love me, right?"

His smile widened. "Right."

And then he kissed me again. And as he did, I suddenly realized something. Had he just confessed that he loved me?

CHAPTER 26

*E*mmanuella Sheetenhelm walked out of the elevator and onto the floor of Jarrett's suite with a swing in her step. She tossed her platinum hair across her shoulder, adjusted the strap of her Louis Vuitton purse and decided to pretend that the stretch of corridor that divided her from the door to the suite was a runway lined with eager spectators, and that she was a model about to launch the new Calvin Klein collection.

She strutted her stuff like a seasoned pro, the flesh-colored Calvin Klein dress swishing about her long legs, the Jimmy Choos traversing the distance with class and style, and her classic features, with her trademark razor-sharp cheekbones, lit up by a happy glow.

She'd just gone shopping with her ex-and-future-husband Broderick's credit card, and had picked out her Vera Wang wedding dress for her upcoming nuptials so she was in a glad, glad mood. She'd divorced Darian's father when rumor had reached her ear about his affair with some young yoga teacher, but that had all been just that: a malicious rumor, so now the marriage was back on, and she got to have a second chance at organizing a fabulous wedding which she wasn't going to say no to.

And she'd just walked out of Harvey Nichols when she'd remembered the text Harry had sent her. The darling girl was apparently busy hosting the Piquant Pack at Jarrett's place, and had texted her to drop by if she could spare a minute, as she needed her help ASAP.

Spending a leisurely afternoon at the Ritz-Carlton in the company of that iconic girl band was not something she was going to thumb her nose at, so she'd ordered the cab driver to take her there pronto and now here she was, about to make her grand entrance.

And she'd only placed her finger on the buzzer when the door suddenly slammed open and a harried-looking woman strode out, her face a thundercloud, and muttering, "Never again! Never again will I set foot in this hellhole!"

"Hey, aren't you Maggie Smith?" she asked when recognition dawned, but the woman simply ignored her and stalked off in the direction of the bank of elevators.

She decided to let herself in and was surprised when a second woman almost bumped into her on her way out. She had a blank look on her face, as if she was sleepwalking or something, and looked vaguely familiar. She was tall and powerfully built, with those square shoulders you often see in Olympic athletes and Madonna.

"Have to... go and... confess..." the woman was mumbling, before following in Maggie Smith's footsteps and stalking off down the corridor.

"Hey, aren't you Courtney Coppola?" she asked, finally remembering where she'd seen that face before. "I love your singing, Courtney," she yelled after the woman.

In spite of these curious meetings, her good humor remained firmly in place, as is to be expected from a woman who's just dropped a few thousand pounds on a wedding dress and a pair of new Jimmy Choos. In fact nothing could put a dent in her mood, not even the quarreling women in the living room. She recognized them as the other four members of the Piquant Pack, and by the looks of it they'd had some sort of falling-out.

"I hate you!" Carrie screamed at Janell.

"And I hate you!" Janell screamed at Carrie.

"I should never have listened to you. Getting back together was the worst idea ever!"

"Then you shouldn't have said yes and signed the bloody contract, you freak!"

Amaryllis was sobbing uncontrollably, rocking herself on the couch, and Perpetua was doing her nails, seemingly unaffected by all the drama.

"Now I remember why I was so happy to quit—I hated you then and I hate you even more now!" Carrie screeched, and launched herself at Janell, nails out. And then they were actually fighting! Rolling on the floor and clawing at each other!

Amaryllis began to sob even louder, hugging herself while she rocked faster, and Perpetua heaved an annoyed sigh while she did another nail.

"Oh dear," muttered Em. She disliked drama, especially when she wasn't the one engaging in it. She decided to sidestep the Piquant Pack and go in search of Harry or Jarrett or one of the other inmates. "Harry?" she called out, checking the kitchen. "Jarrett?" She briefly took a peek inside the bedrooms—which were all in a terrible state—and then cracked open the door to the bathroom. "Deshawn? Where are you?" The second bathroom yielded no results either, but by now it had become obvious to her why Harry had sent out that distress signal: the suite was an absolute shambles!

Clothes were strewn all over the place, the floors were littered with brassieres, knickers, makeup items, pizza boxes, fast food cartons, candy wrappers, and even a butcher knife carelessly left lying around underneath the couch. And as she started picking up stuff here and there, her eye was drawn to absolutely the most hideous artifacts she'd ever seen in her life.

She cried out in horror, her equanimity disturbed for the first time since she's set foot inside the suite. And the more she looked, the more of these horrible things she found. They were simply everywhere!

A look of resolution stole over her face. She was a woman on a mission. As a patron of the arts, and a person with a keen eye for beauty and artistry, she could not condone this-this abomination! Her own apartment was a temple of esthetics, filled with little knickknacks and pretty baubles she'd picked up on her travels and frequent visits to antique stores all over the city. This crime against good taste would not stand.

When finally she'd gone through all the rooms, she'd removed no less than thirty of those fake hideous amulets. They all dangled from her hands from those horrid red cords. Pressing her lips together with determination, she stalked from the suite, and dumped all of them in the bin closest to the elevators. And as she did, she rubbed her hands once and with pride. "There," she murmured. "One good deed done."

And then she returned to the suite—to continue her efforts to clean out this pigsty. How Jarrett, Deshawn and Harry had allowed things to go so wrong so fast was beyond her. Good thing she was here now. Soon the suite would be up to Ritz standards once again.

CHAPTER 27

"One of the Piquant Pack is here to see you, sir," said Tilda, popping her head in.

"Which one?"

"Courtney, sir."

"Right," he said knowingly. If someone had told him he'd become a Piquant Pack cognoscente, he'd never have believed them. "Show her in."

He tidied up his desk a little. Then he adjusted his tie and wiped his lips with the back of his hand to make sure there weren't any crumbs left from that roast duck sandwich he'd just polished off. When Courtney walked in, he got up courteously. "Miss Coppola."

She didn't seem herself as she took a seat. "I did it," she announced.

"You did what?" he asked pleasantly.

Then she looked straight at him, and said, "I killed Aldo Brookfield. I dealt him the killing blow."

"Um, wait—what?" he asked, taken aback.

"We all killed him," she continued, speaking in a strange,

detached voice. "We're all equally to blame. Amaryllis, Janell, Carrie, Perpetua and me."

"You're not serious."

"I am very serious. And I want you to record my confession so there can be no doubt. And I want you to arrest the others, too, and lock us all up in jail for the rest of our lives. We're murderers. Cold-blooded killers. We murdered an innocent man—a man who dedicated his life to our success. Who gave up everything so we could become the biggest female band in the history of this country. A man who worked tirelessly for our benefit, and took nothing in return. A man, in short, who was a genuine hero. And what did we do to thank him? We knocked his block off. Just because he showed us some genuine affection. Was that fair? Was that nice? No, it was not."

"I—I—I..." Darian sat back, robbed of speech. His hands flew to his neatly combed hair, and he dug his fingers in, pulling vigorously. What the hell?!

"I want you to arrest me, Inspector Watley. And I want you to do more. I also want you to arrest Henrietta McCabre and Jarrett Zephyr-Thornton. Because they knew about this terrible crime and they didn't come forward and report it to you. They're complicit in their silence and I'm sure there's some kind of punishment for that kind of thing, too."

Darian narrowed his eyes at Courtney. "Are you on drugs?"

"No, I'm not, Inspector. I'm of sound mind and body and I'm confessing to have committed a terrible, terrible crime."

Then it suddenly dawned on him. "You're Aldo, aren't you? You've jumped out of Deshawn's body and now you've jumped into Courtney's. You're making her do this!"

"I don't know what you're talking about, Inspector," said Courtney, still in that strangely detached voice. "My name is

Courtney Coppola and I'm a murderer. Please arrest me and get this over with."

He nodded. "Very well. Why don't you go cool your heels in a cell?" And he called in Tilda to take Courtney down to the cell block in the basement. The moment they were gone, he called Harry on her cell. "Harry? I need you down here. Courtney just confessed. And I'm pretty sure she's possessed by Aldo."

❧

It took us all of twenty minutes to return to Scotland Yard. We were almost home after our visit to Deshawn, but that was before Darian had announced that Courtney had turned herself in. When we arrived in Darian's office, he was pacing the small space like a caged tiger. His hair, usually so nicely in place, was a mess. When we entered his office, he turned on us with a vengeance. "What took you so long?!"

"Traffic," said Jarrett with a nasty gleam in his eye. On the ride over, he'd suddenly decided that if Darian really wanted to, he could release Deshawn. When I tried to explain to him that Commissioner Slack didn't want Deshawn released, and that if Darian signed the release order, he'd probably be arrested himself, he refused to accept that 'lame excuse.'

"Courtney just arrived. She confessed to killing Aldo. She also said the others are equally to blame. They were all in it together. Can you believe it?!"

"I can," said Jarrett. "And you probably arrested her, didn't you? That's what you do. You just arrest and arrest and arrest and then pretend it's not your fault. You know what you are, sir? A compulsive arrester."

Darian cut his eyes to me, and I shrugged. Jarrett was in

one of his moods again. "So what are you going to do?" I asked.

"What can I do? She insisted she wanted to be arrested—she and her bandmates—and thrown in jail for the rest of their lives!"

"Where is she now?"

"Downstairs. In one of the cells."

"Where you keep all of your prisoners," said Jarrett nastily. "In a place cold and dark and probably infested with thousands of spiders and rats and other vermin of the underground." He uttered a muffled sob. "Poor Deshawn. He's probably terrified by now."

"Um, actually it's pretty clean down there," said Darian. "They remodeled this entire building before moving us in. It's not the Ritz, of course, but it's clean and dry. And completely free of rats and spiders and other vermin."

"Let's take a look," I suggested. And as we followed Darian out of his office, I said, "Nice office, by the way."

"It's not mine," he said gloomily. "The only person in the entire building who has his own office is Slack. The rest of us have to snap up what we can when we arrive in the morning."

"A little bit like Deshawn once you put him in general population," said Jarrett. "Where he will have to fend for himself and create a shank so he can fight for his life."

"It's not like that," Darian assured him.

"That's what you say," Jarrett muttered darkly.

"Look, what can I do? He attacked a woman in front of the bloody Queen!"

Jarrett narrowed his eyes at him. "I'll bet you can do plenty, Inspector Watley." And with these words, he turned on his heel and strode off.

"Jarrett!" Darian yelled.

"What?!" Jarrett responded without looking back.

"It's this way."

Jarrett performed a U-turn in the narrow corridor and sailed right back. "You did that on purpose," he said.

"I did what on purpose?!"

"Sent me down the rabbit hole. You probably hoped I'd get lost. Well, I'm here to tell you that you will never get rid of me, Inspector Watley. I'll be on you like white on rice until you release my boyfriend!"

"Back off, Zephyr," Darian growled, and I watched as both men went toe to toe. It was a curious sight: the tough cop and the effeminate fop.

If the situation wasn't as serious as it was, I would have thought the whole thing hilarious. Now, though, I said, "Don't let Aldo turn you against each other. Don't you see? This is what he does. He turns friends into enemies."

"I'm not backing down," said Jarrett, still nose to nose with Darian.

"Me neither," said Darian. "Tell your colleague to stand down, Harry."

"Come on, you guys. We don't have time for this nonsense."

"Stand down, Watley. I'm warning you," Jarrett grunted.

"You stand down, Zephyr."

"Zephyr-Thornton the Third."

"I don't bloody care!"

"Oi!" I shouted. Both men looked up. "Cut it out!"

Finally, reason seemed to return to its throne, as both men relented.

"This isn't over, Watley," Jarrett said, having to get the last word in.

We rode the elevator down in silence, the hostility between the two men creating a tense atmosphere you could cut with a knife. The elevator jerked to a stop and we got out, Darian leading the way.

"Be cool," I hissed when Jarrett fell into step beside me.

"I'll be cool when he's cool!"

"I think he's being pretty damned cool—he could have arrested Courtney and the others but instead he chose to call us!"

This gave Jarrett pause for a moment, but then he said, "Or maybe this is all a trick and he's going to arrest us next!"

I shook my head, raising my eyes ceilingward. We'd arrived at the cell block, and after negotiating safe passage with the guards on duty, we followed Darian inside the small space. "Is Deshawn still here?" asked Jarrett.

"He is," Darian confirmed. "They're picking him up in an hour or so for transport to Pentonville Prison."

A sobbing sound escaped Jarrett's throat, and I patted his back consolingly. "You better tell him to start working on that shank."

We stood in front of the cell that held Courtney, only one set of vertical iron bars between us. The woman had turned her back on us. "Courtney," I said. "We're here to take you home."

She glanced over her shoulder. "I'm here to stay. I'm a murderer, remember?"

"No, you're not," I said. "What you are is possessed by Aldo Brookfield."

The woman's face twisted into a grimace. "You don't say."

"Yes, I do say. So get out of Courtney, Aldo, or I'll kick you out."

I had no idea how to go about that, but my intention must have shone through my words loud and clear, for suddenly the ghost of Aldo Brookfield left Courtney's body and floated through the bars in our direction. "I won, you stupid woman. I won!"

"No, you didn't," I said as I darted a quick look at Courtney, who'd sagged on the bench inside her cell. She looked confused, as she would be, after this ordeal.

"What's going on?" asked Deshawn, who was in the next cell.

"Deshawn!" cried Jarrett happily. "You're still alive!"

"My previous host," said Aldo with an evil grin. "You served me well, Mr. Little. Though you should stop grinding your teeth so much. You'll wear them down."

"See?!" Jarrett exclaimed. "I told you you grind your teeth but you wouldn't believe me!"

"Oh, he does a lot more than grind his teeth," said Aldo. "For one thing, he manscapes! Oh, the horror!"

"There's nothing wrong with manscaping," said Deshawn, unperturbed.

"Yes, I manscape," said Jarrett. "It's a sign of respect for your lover, isn't that right, lover?"

"It most certainly is," Deshawn confirmed. "And I hope to keep up the habit in Pentonville Prison, my next destination."

"When you take a shower, just be careful never to bend over and pick up the soap, darling," said Jarrett with a sob. "Watch your back!"

"Oh, cut the crap," said Aldo. "I've got you all where I want you." He turned to Darian. "Arrest these two bozos, Inspector. They knew my five girls murdered me and they refused to report it to the police. That's punishable behavior in my book."

"I'll decide who to arrest," said Darian, directing a dark look at the manager. "And right now, I think it's safe to say that Courtney Coppola was acting under extreme duress when she confessed to me, so I'm going to disregard her confession and have her released. Besides, the Aldo Brookfield murder is solved already. Jamil Dove murdered you."

"Who?!"

Darian smiled. "A character almost as unpleasant as yourself."

"You can't do that!"

"I already have."

"Oh, you think you're clever, huh?! I'll just possess Courtney again and confess to some other cop, cop!"

"No, you won't," I said, posting myself in front of the horrible ghost. "Before you possess that woman again, you'll have to go through me."

"Oh, with pleasure," he said, and dove straight through me, en route to Courtney. But before he could get there, Jarrett was waiting for him. "And what do you want, you stupid fop?"

"Recognize this?" asked Jarrett, and suddenly took one of Evette's amulets from his pocket and dangled it in Aldo's face. Instantly, the ghost reeled back.

"That's not fair!" he cried. "Put that away!"

But instead of putting it away, Jarrett stepped closer to the ghost, holding out the amulet in front of him like a banner. "What is it, Aldo? Afraid of a little gold coin?"

The ghost's face was contorted in rage as he recoiled further and further. "I'll get you for this! I'll get you all—you included, you backstabbing copper!"

And with these final words, he suddenly dove into the cement walls of the underground cell block, and disappeared from view.

CHAPTER 28

We decided the time had come to visit Magical Mages once again. Evette's idea about the circle had backfired, since Aldo had been inside Deshawn at the time, and he would hardly be lured into the circle since he now knew all about it. There was only one thing for it: Evette would have to come up with another plan.

Unfortunately, when we arrived at the store, a big sign on the door announced that it was closed for the day. Bummer. And of course I didn't have Evette's number.

"Nobody says no to a Zephyr-Thornton," said Jarrett, and rattled the door for good measure. When that didn't help, he proceeded to tap on the window until the single pane shook.

"I don't think she's here, Jarrett."

"She must be here," he said through gritted teeth. "We need her. If she's as good as she says she is, she knows we need her and she gives us another crack at this Aldo character."

"Or maybe she knew we were coming and decided we didn't need her."

"What are you talking about? Of course we need her. We can't pull this off without her. She knows that!"

"Maybe we can. Maybe we can do more than we give ourselves credit for."

"I don't know what you're talking about, Harry. I for one have no idea how to handle this Aldo. In fact the more we're sinking into this Piquant Pack quagmire, the more I'm starting to think we're not up to the task."

"Oh, but we are," I said, suddenly filled with a renewed sense of purpose. "So far we've managed to keep the girls out of prison, haven't we?"

"And have landed one of our own inside it," he reminded me.

"Yes," I admitted. "That was a setback."

"A setback?! Deshawn will rot in jail for the rest of his life!"

"I'm sure the Queen will manage to get him out."

"Well, I'm glad your confidence in Our Majesty is rock solid, as I'm not so sure myself. She has to set an example, Harry. She can't go around pardoning murderous maniacs. No, Deshawn is going to be in that penitentiary for a very long time to come." He sank back against his Rolls and crossed his arms forlornly. "And I'm going to be husbandless for the same amount of time. Which is a shame, really. Ours could have been one of those epic relationships. The ones that stand the test of time. Like Samson and Delilah. Or Cleopatra and Mark Antony. Or even George and Kenny."

"I think you should aim higher, Jarrett. All those relationships ended in disaster. Do you really want to follow in their footsteps? I think love should be a happy thing, right? Not a disastrous affair."

He nodded, a ponderous look on his face. "Why don't we simply spring Deshawn from jail? Bust him out? Or, better yet, hijack the prison transfer. Darian told us they're shipping him to Pentonville Prison. We can rescue him."

"I don't think that's such a good idea, Jarrett. We're in enough trouble as it is, without trying to break Deshawn from prison."

His shoulders stooped. "You're probably right. We would need Dwayne Johnson and Vin Diesel to pull off such a stunt, and they're not in my Rolodex, I'm afraid."

It was a sad couple of Wraith Wranglers who made their way home in Jarrett's Rolls. And to make matters worse, Buckley was once again nowhere to be seen. Obviously he felt that we didn't need him at this, our hour of need, but he was wrong. We needed all the help we could get. And by the time we rode the elevator up to Jarrett's suite, I'd already come up with and discarded so many plans that I was at the end of my rope. It had sounded pretty good, that wheeze about not needing Evette, but who was I kidding? We were outghosted, and that was the plain truth.

When we arrived at the door to the suite, a voice arrested our attention. It belonged to none other than Marisol Glee, the famous diva with the voice of an angel. She came tripping in our direction on high heels, looking jazzed up. "Oh, hi, Miss McCabre—Mr. Zephyr. Is it true that the Piquant Pack are currently staying in your suite?"

"That's right," said Jarrett, his frown quickly turning into a smile when he recognized the diva. "Miss Glee. It's an honor to finally meet you."

"We met before," she reminded him. She'd squeezed her ample assets into a tight black sequined dress that barely covered both her hips and her bosom, and had allowed her long, golden hair to fall unfettered across her bare shoulders. She was shorter than me, I discovered, something I hadn't noticed when watching her perform on TV.

"Did we?" asked Jarrett. "Never in person. I would remember."

She giggled at the compliment. "I was on the Graham Norton Show. You were in the audience. And I was at the awards ceremony at Buckingham Palace. Before your friend went berserk and was arrested."

The fact seemed to give her some satisfaction, and now I remembered she'd been upstaged by Deshawn on both occasions. For a diva of her standing, the fact must not have gone down well.

"So to what do I owe the pleasure?" asked Jarrett, valiantly resisting the powerful urge to defend Deshawn.

"I'm going on tour again. Just a small one. Wembley Stadium. Royal Albert Hall. The O2. And I wanted to ask the girls to do my opening act."

"They just quit," I said.

"I know! I saw that. Such a shame. I'm hoping to convince them otherwise."

"Well, you never know," I admitted while Jarrett opened the door. "I've tried to change their mind, but they seem pretty adamant about throwing in the towel."

"Let me have a go at them," said Marisol, planning her hands on her hips. "I can be pretty convincing if I want to be."

Judging from the resolute look on her face, she wasn't lying. And I'd just opened the door when suddenly, out of nowhere, the ghost of Aldo Brookfield zoomed into view, and dove into the body of the famous diva!

CHAPTER 29

We half stumbled, half fell into the suite, and as I tried to stop Marisol, Jarrett had the same idea and we both ended up clawing at thin air and tripping each other up.

"Hey, girls," said Marisol brightly as she entered the living room.

"Stop!" I shouted as I scrambled to my feet. "Stop her!"

The five members of the Piquant Pack were seated in a circle, obviously holding some kind of meeting, and looked up in surprise when we interrupted their quiet time.

"What's going on?" asked Janell. Then, as she recognized Marisol, her expression changed. "Marisol Glee! Oh, this is such an honor!"

"Stop her! She's not Marisol!" I yelled.

"Well, she is Marisol, only she isn't," Jarrett explained, scrabbling in on hands and feet.

"We were just having a moment to restore peace amongst ourselves," Janell explained.

"Yes, there's been so much fighting going on," said

Amaryllis, darting an accusatory glance at Carrie and Janell, "that it's time to be friends again."

Janell squeezed Carrie's hand. "We're good now, though, aren't we, Carrie?"

"Yes, we are," said Carrie with an apologetic smile. "I don't know what came over me. We never used to fight like that before. I love you, Janell."

"Oh, and I love you, sweetie," said Janell, and gave her a hug.

Meanwhile, Marisol had snuck off, and I feared the worst. "Look, it's great that you're making up and all, but you have to watch out for Marisol. She's—"

"Just about the biggest singer the world has ever seen," said Amaryllis. "Yay!"

"No, but she's—"

"I wanted to thank you guys," said Courtney, "for what you did for me back there. If not for you, I'd be in jail right now, and so would the rest of us. You saved my life."

"You're welcome," said Jarrett, unashamedly taking the credit for Courtney's narrow escape. "I had to reason with Inspector Watley, of course. You know the type. Too stubborn to look for the truth."

"Jarrett," I warned him.

"Then again, he did agree pretty quickly to let you go," he said. "Which just goes to show that even amongst Scotland Yard, some minds are quicker than others. Though as long as he doesn't let Deshawn go," he added with a nasty look at me, "I'm still holding him responsible when the love of my life gets shanked in the gizzard."

And then I saw it: Marisol had returned, and this time she was holding a very large butcher's knife. The kind that can do some real damage. The cruel smile on her lips said it all. "Hi, girls. Look what I got here."

There was a squeal of surprise from Amaryllis. "Did you

bring us a present?"

"Oh, yes, I did," said Marisol, and then her voice magically morphed into Aldo's. "And now I'm going to let you have it!" And she lunged at the nearest Piquant Pack member, which was Courtney! The latter deftly parried the thrust by throwing a side table at Marisol. The knife clattered to the floor and skittered underneath the sofa, and Marisol snarled, "That won't save you, my dear Courtney!" And she went down on all fours to retrieve the knife.

"I thought he couldn't attack us with all those amulets?!" Jarrett cried.

I glanced around, and noticed for the first time the tidiness of the suite. And the lack of amulets! "They're gone! They're all gone!"

"Some lady was in here," Amaryllis explained. "She said they were beyond ugly and threw them all out."

"What lady? Grace?"

"No, Grace left. Told me to tell you she quit," Janell said. "She couldn't stand the mess and the noise and the screaming and the drama. Said we were worse than children."

I dove for Marisol, landed on her back, and tried to hold her down. She was surprisingly strong for a woman her size, though, and threw me off with a loud snarl. I saw she'd gotten hold of the knife and was approaching the five women, a leering grin on her face. I'd never seen Marisol like this before, and the effect was disconcerting to say the least.

The five women cowered, and in an effort to stop the maniac, I picked up a pouffe and threw it at Marisol's back. It connected and she went down again, the knife dropping inside the circle of women. They all stared at it, as if it was a snake, and then Carrie gave it a vicious kick that sent it flying through the air, and hitting a Warholian-style painting of Deshawn and Jarrett. And there it stayed, buried in Jarrett's face.

With an almost animal roar, Marisol reared up again and staggered in the direction of the five women. I dove for her feet, but she kicked me, hard. Her foot connected with my shoulder and I was spun around and away.

"Jarrett! Do something!" I yelled as I landed on my hip.

Jarrett seemed unsure how to approach the situation. "But I'm a fan," he said desperately.

"She's not Marisol right now! She's Aldo!"

That seemed to decide Jarrett, for he walked up to Marisol, hauled off, and hit her smack dab in the face with a right hook. Blood spurted from the diva's wounded schnoz and she was catapulted back, straight into the heart of the circle of women. And that's when an idea occurred to me.

"Join me!" I yelled to Jarrett, and scooted over between Janell and Carrie, taking their hands.

"Oh, I see what you're trying to do," said Janell, and gave my hand a happy squeeze.

Jarrett had also caught on, and now took a seat between Amaryllis and Perpetua. The circle was closed, and Marisol was sitting in the middle, gingerly touching her nose. Had Aldo left her body? Was the diva herself again? We watched with bated breath. But then the singer's face clouded, and she snarled, "This dumb circle can't hold me!" And she made to break through the hands closing the circle.

Just at that moment, however, the door to the suite swung open, and Em appeared, her arms bedecked with dozens of amulets. "Oh, you guys, I'd already thrown these out before it struck me that they might have some emotional value or something. So here they are." She'd approached us and was eyeing the circle a little strangely. "Hey, is that Marisol Glee?" she asked, then her expression of surprise turned into one of upset. "And have you punched her in the face?!"

Marisol, who'd been on the verge of leaving the circle of women—and one man—was struck back by the force that emanated from the amulets, and with a shriek of horror dropped back down to the floor. "Get those away from me!" she yelled.

"What—these?" asked Em, holding up the collection of amulets. "Oh, I see what you mean. I had the same reaction myself. They are pretty horrid, aren't they? A crime against esthetics."

At this, I decided now was the time to recite those lines Evette had taught us, so I said, "Oh, spirit evil as demons three—go now and leave us be—return to hell we beg of thee—spirits good and true cannot you see—get rid of Aldo Brookfield and set us free!"

The others all joined in, even as Em muttered, "Now—really!"

"Oh, spirit evil as demons three—go now and leave us be—return to hell we beg of thee—spirits good and true cannot you see—get rid of Aldo Brookfield and set us free!"

Over and over again, we repeated the phrase, louder and louder, and suddenly, out of nowhere, angelic figures seemed to drift down from the ceiling, taking a look at what was going on down here. In the heart of the circle, Marisol watched it all with a look of abject fear on her face. "No, no, no, no, no!" she cried. "You can't do this to me!"

We ignored his pleading and continued our chant, and as more and more of those cherubic figures joined us and started darting across the room, suddenly the strangest thing happened: the soul of Aldo Brookfield seemed to detach itself from Marisol's body, as if it was being sucked right out of it, and then, with a loud agonized wail, suddenly the angelic beings pounced on the defenseless manager, and started dragging him away. A wind had come up, and was whipping at my face and my clothes and making my eyes water.

"You have to close a window," said Em. "There's a nasty

draft in here."

"I'll get you for this!" Aldo screamed. "Just you wait and see! This isn't over!"

They were his last words, for the next moment, he was dragged down and abruptly disappeared into the floor, almost as if he was tipped off a cliff and chucked into the abyss. There was a loud cry of anguish, and after what seemed like an eternity, the cry ended. As abruptly as it had come up, the howling wind died down again, and with it, the angelic emanation also disappeared. When Em finally returned, announcing she'd closed the bedroom window, silence had returned.

In the heart of the circle, Marisol sat blinking confusedly, then reached for her nose. "Ouch. What happened? How did I suddenly move from the hallway to here?"

"Oh, Marisol," said Amaryllis with a laugh. "You're back!"

"I was never gone," said the diva, looking perplexed.

The women all hugged each other, including Marisol in the hug, and Jarrett and I also shared in the relief. "Is he gone?" asked Courtney. "Is he really gone?"

"Yes, he is," I said. "He's finally gone for good."

"Thank you," she breathed, and squeezed me so hard I groaned.

"Who's gone?" asked Em. "And who broke Marisol's nose?"

"My nose is broken?!" Marisol yelped.

"Oh, it's not broken," Jarrett assured her. "Just a minor scratch."

Just then, another figure came flying into the room. It was Buckley, and when he saw us all looking back at him, he asked, a little sheepishly, "Did I miss something? I did, didn't I? It's just that I just spent the day inhabiting the body of the Prime Minister. It was so much fun! I signed at least a dozen new laws, increasing the minimum wage, funding for the

NHS, new scholarships, improving and expanding maternity leave..." His voice trailed off. "I really did miss something, didn't I? Something important."

"Well, turning England into a socialist paradise is probably important, too," I said, "but yes, you did miss something. You missed us vanquishing the evil spirit of Aldo Brookfield, and sending him back to where he belongs."

"To hell," Janell said with a happy grin.

"Oh, dear," said Buckley, pressing a hand to his cheek.

"We managed, Buckley," said Jarrett. "Though next time it would be nice if you could lend a helping hand when we're battling a murderous maniacal manager."

"Let's hope there won't be a next time," said Amaryllis, then added, with sparkling eyes, "You know what this means, don't you?"

"I'm suing you for battery and assault," asked Marisol, then smiled, and amended, "Just kidding. Though I am sending you my plastic surgeon's bill and it won't be cheap."

"We're getting the band back together!" cried Amaryllis, jumping up and down.

"Are you sure?" asked Carrie uncertainly. "Look what happened the last time."

"I think we should give it another shot," Janell said. "Besides, with Harry and Jarrett by our side, what could happen?"

And so it was decided. After getting back together and breaking up again, the Piquant Pack was staging another comeback. "Can I be your special guest?" asked Marisol, who was dabbing at her nose with a handkerchief Em had handed her.

"Of course you can!" Amaryllis yelled. "Piquant Pack featuring Marisol! This is going to be big, you guys!"

"Just like my nose," said Marisol with a frown as she assessed the damage in a pocket mirror.

EPILOGUE

We were back at the Graham Norton Show, only this time Jarrett and I weren't in the audience. We were actually on stage, sitting on those famous red couches right next to Graham Norton himself! We weren't alone, of course. Janell, Amaryllis, Perpetua, Courtney and Carrie were also there, and so was Marisol Glee!

And as I glanced into the audience, I was happy to find Darian and his mum and dad giving me an enthusiastic thumbs-up, as were Jarrett's folks. The only one who wasn't there was Buckley, but that was probably because he was currently trying to jump into the skin of Bill Gates, persuading the billionaire to use his billions to make the world a better place.

"The Wraith Wranglers. This is such a joy," said Graham as he beamed at us. "I've heard the Piquant Pack are your latest clients, and that they couldn't be happier with the service you provided. Is that right, ladies?"

"These two are simply amazing," Janell gushed. "We had a

ghost problem and they fixed it—like that!" She snapped her fingers.

"Yeah, we love them," Amaryllis added.

"Whenever you have a ghost issue, they're the ones to call," said Courtney.

"The only ones to call," Carrie stressed.

"And they're great people, too," Perpetua said with a rare smile.

"The best!" Amaryllis yelled.

"I hear you," said Graham. "And whenever some old ghoul gets under my skin, you're the guys I'll call in. In fact you're on speed dial these days!"

"Why, thank you, Graham," said Jarrett. "That's very gratifying to hear."

"But there's a third member who's absent right now, isn't there?"

"Yes, there is," said Jarrett, his face falling. "My boyfriend Deshawn."

"The great cake baker. He's in prison, facing a long stretch for disturbing the peace at the Queen's latest birthday honors."

"Yes, we've tried everything," I said, "but Deshawn is still in prison."

"There has even been a petition on Change.org," said Graham, "but that hasn't done much to convince the authorities that they've made a grave mistake, has it?"

"Unfortunately not," I agreed.

"It's a gross miscarriage of justice," said Jarrett. "Deshawn had nothing to do with that whole mess at Buckingham Palace."

"Yes, you claim he was possessed by a ghost, right?"

"Well, he was."

"Yes, he most certainly was," said Amaryllis. "And I should know, as he was coming after me!"

"Well, then what I'm about to tell you will make you all very happy," said Graham with a twinkle in his eye. "Because it has behooved Her Royal Highness to issue a royal pardon to Deshawn Little, and he's joining us here now—fresh out of Pentonville Prison!"

And to loud cheers and applause, Deshawn walked out onto the stage!

"Deshawn!" cried Jarrett, popping up from his seat like a happy flea. "You're free!"

"Yes, I am," said Deshawn, who looked skinnier than before but much happier than when we'd seen him last. And then both men fell into each other's arms and kissed, right in front of the cameras and a whooping studio audience.

And as if that wasn't enough, Darian took advantage of the general confusion to mount the stage in three long strides and scoop me up in his arms and plant a hot kiss on my lips as well.

"Hey, you're not a Wraith Wrangler!" Graham yelled.

"He's an honorary member!" I yelled back, and that's exactly what he was. Too late I remembered Darian's desire to fly under the radar, so as not to get into trouble with Commissioner Slack and his colleagues. Oops!

"Oh, to hell with it," Darian declared. "I'm a Wraith Wrangler, too."

And then there was a lot more kissing, and even a performance by the Piquant Pack, featuring Marisol Glee, sporting a brand-new and improved nose. And as we enjoyed the show, Graham Norton sidled up to me. "If you have a minute, could I have a word with you guys after the show? A ghost has been infesting this studio for ages and simply refuses to leave, the crusty old bugger. Could you…"

Jarrett and Darian and Deshawn and I shared a grin. "Of course we can!"

THE END

Thanks for reading! If you want to know when a new Nic Saint book comes out, sign up for Nic's mailing list: nicsaint.com/news

EXCERPT FROM GHOSTLIER THINGS (GHOSTS OF LONDON 6)

Chapter One

"So you and a copper, eh?" asked my friend, darting a look of admiration over her cup of tea. "Scotland Yard man no less. Who would have thought?"

"Definitely not me," I intimated with a shrug.

Mavis Bletchley had been my best friend in high school, and even though we hadn't seen each other in ages, the moment we did, it was just like old times.

She was a red-haired slightly overweight woman, large-framed glasses obscuring the better part of her face, as they had done all through high school, lively blue eyes perpetually in wonder about what was going in the world around her.

I liked Mavis. Always had. We'd been seated next to each other all through the upper grades and had had each other's back when the bullying was hard and relentless, as it invariably is when a bunch of girls are forced to spend every waking hour together.

"Is he nice? Is he handsome? Is he sexy?" Her eyes

widened. "Is he rich, like good old Mr. Darcy? Has he proposed yet? Given you a big rock of a ring?"

I giggled. This was regular girl's talk, the sort of thing I hadn't engaged in for a long time, and the kind of stuff I now realized I'd missed.

I sat a little straighter, and held my own cup of tea a little tighter. "He's very nice, he's very handsome, he's... not really very rich but he does own an entire apartment block so he's definitely not poor. And even though he hasn't proposed yet I think he just might. He seems to think I'm the one."

"And do you think he's the one?" Mavis asked with bated breath, then blew it out across her steaming cup of Earl Grey tea.

"Yes, actually I do. I do think he's the one. Oh, you should have seen him when he had to get me out of a fix the last time, Mavis. Like a real hero."

"A regular knight in shining armor, then, eh?"

"Something like that. He is very chivalrous."

"Not like those blokes down at the Bell's Whistle who are always trying to get into my knickers. They're regular pests. Have to tell 'em off every time."

"No, he's not that kind of bloke," I admitted. "Far from it, in fact."

Mavis and I were seated on the little balcony of the flat she rented in Catford, in South East London. It was a little ways away from my own modest flat in West London, so I'd had to take the Tube and a short walk across the London Bridge to get here. It was definitely worth it, though, to see my old high school bestie again.

Mavis now worked as a cashier in her local Lidl, even though her dream had been to become the first female Prime Minister of Britain. I'd always told her Maggie had beaten her to the punch, but she didn't care. Mavis was stubborn that way. How she was going to go from cashier to PM I didn't know, and I had a sneaking suspicion she didn't either. But that didn't stop her from holding on to her dream.

"Want another slice?" she asked now, gesturing at the small array of crumbs which was all that was left of my sticky toffee cake.

"Well…" I rubbed my tummy, then relented. "Don't mind if I do, actually."

"I get them with my employee discount card. Ten percent off and even twenty percent at Christmas." She darted a slightly envious look at my flat belly. "How do you manage to stay so slim? You haven't changed a bit since graduation. In fact you look even skinnier now than you did five years ago."

I shrugged. "Good genes?"

"That must be it. My genes are simply terrible. Every pound I eat sticks to my hips and magically turns into two pounds added to the scale." She got up and moved into the small kitchen adjacent to the balcony. "One thick slice of sticky toffee cake coming up!" she yelled. "More tea, Harry?"

"No, thanks, I'm fine."

"It's great tea. Big on quality, Lidl on price!" she caroled.

"You should join the marketing department!" I yelled back.

It was a nice day, the sun having risen high on the firmament. Beneath my feet a peaceful neighborhood stretched out, one of the last neighborhoods where property prices hadn't soared. Mavis lived just around the corner from the giant one-story high fiberglass Catford Cat which adorned the local KFC.

It was nice to have a day off for once. Recently the ghost hunting business I'd launched with my best friend Jarrett Zephyr-Thornton had been a roaring success. Especially since we'd helped the Piquant Pack, the most popular girl band for the last two decades, vanquish the ghost of their former manager.

A gentle breeze ruffled my short blond tresses and I closed my eyes to enjoy the feel of the sunshine on my face, warming me up.

"Let them eat cake!" Mavis shouted, shoving a really big chunk of the stuff onto my plate. I wasn't going to stay slim if I kept indulging in Mavis's cake. Then again, I deserved it. The Wraith Wranglers had solved a couple of high-profile cases lately, and I enjoyed the vacation from wrangling ghosts.

"So wraith wrangling, huh?" asked Mavis. "Do you really believe in all of that ghost stuff or is it just for show? Please be honest with me, Harry."

"Of course I believe in that stuff," I said, cutting off a piece of the creamy rich cake with my fork. "I wouldn't be much of a ghost hunter if I didn't."

"No, but I mean—ghosts don't really exist, do they? They're just a figment of our imagination. You can tell me, Harry. We've been friends for ages." She gave me a wink while stuffing a big piece of cake into her mouth. "I won't spill your secrets to the tabloids, I swear."

"Ghosts exist, Mavis. No, they really do."

"But what about that stuff you pulled off at the Graham Norton Show? That was just a hoax, right? When that so-called ghost dropped down those lights on the Piquant Pack and started yelling about taking revenge?"

I smiled. It was obvious Mavis was one of those people who didn't believe in ghosts, and that was fine with me. I hadn't believed in ghosts before my ex-employer Geoffrey Buckley was murdered and his ghost returned from the dead to help me solve his murder. Now? I sometimes felt London housed more ghosts than living people—and they were all clamoring for my help.

"Ghosts exist," I repeated. "Trust me on that."

She gave me a dubious and slightly hurt look—as if upset

that I refused to confide in an old friend. "If you say so," she said smartly. "You're the expert."

I picked up my cup for another sip, and that's when I felt it. A sudden weakness that seemed to start at my fingers and spread out across my chest. The cup dropped from my hand, and moments later my eyes turned up in my head and I fell, face forward, into the big chunk of cake. The last thing I remembered was the wet squishy feel of the cake on my face, and Mavis screaming, "Harry! Are you all right? Harry! Say something!"

When I regained consciousness, it was with a pounding headache and my face smeared with cake. And when I looked around, weak and nauseous, I saw that I was no longer on the balcony but sitting on the cold kitchen floor. There was a knife in my right hand, and next to me was Mavis's body, lying in a pool of blood, her lifeless eyes staring up at me. And then I screamed.

Chapter Two

"Now this is a nice thing you did to me," a hollow voice spoke. I looked around, and saw that the ghost of Mavis was sitting on top of the kitchen counter, idly swinging her legs and giving me an openly accusatory look.

"Wha-what happened?" I asked.

"You tell me, Harry. One moment I was trying to help you up after you dozed off on top of your cake—a very rude thing to do, I don't mind telling you—and the next thing I know I'm down on the floor and I'm... dead!"

"But..." I stared down at the knife that was still in my hand. It was one of those big butcher knives, sharp as a razor and capable of slicing and dicing anything, including my best friend from high school. "I don't understand."

"Well, I do. You snapped, Harry. I don't know if it's all this wraith wrangling you've been doing—but you snapped and killed me, didn't you?"

"I'm sure I didn't," I said feebly. To be honest I had no recollection of anything past falling face first into a slice of Lidl sticky toffee cake.

"How could you, Harry?" asked Mavis, shaking her head ruefully. "How could you murder your high school bestie? I wasn't ready to die yet."

"I'm sure I didn't do it, Mavis. I would never kill anyone."

"Oh, sure. Just look at me, Harry. Just look at what you did."

I did look, then, and was starting to feel weak at the knees again. This wasn't happening! "But Mavis, I would never—I mean, I'm not—this is impossible!"

"Well, it happened. You murdered me. Now what are you going to do about it?"

I had no idea, actually. No idea how I'd gotten in this situation. Had I blacked out or something? Where did this big bloody knife come from? Why was it in my hand? And how had Mavis ended up dead on the floor?

"I must have blacked out," I said, touching a distraught hand to my face. "And then someone must have snuck in here and killed you. That's the only explanation."

"The only explanation is that you killed me, Harry," said Mavis, giving me a steely look. She flapped her arms. "And now look at me! How am I ever going to become the first female PM now? Dead people don't go into politics, Harry—and they definitely don't get to run the country."

"There's already been two female PMs, Mavis," I countered. I was loathe to argue with my friend, but I couldn't help point out this flaw in her plan.

"Nonsense."

"Margaret Thatcher beat you to it—back in the eighties."

"I'm pretty sure someone would have told me about that."

"And Theresa May? She's a woman."

"I'm pretty sure Theresa May is a bloke."

"Whatever. I hate to tell you this, Mavis, but you were never going to be the first female PM."

"No, that's definitely off the table now, isn't it? No thanks to you. I should have known better than to invite Harry McCabre, famous wraith wrangler, into my home. I should have known you'd go all whacky on me." She shook her head. "This is not the Harry I knew and loved, Harry. You've changed!"

I gave her a feeble smile. "At least you can see I wasn't lying about there being ghosts, right?"

"Ha ha, very funny. I didn't have to find out like this!" She stared down at her hands. "Though it is kinda cool to be a ghost, I have to admit." She jumped off the counter. "So what happens now?"

"Now we have to find your killer and help you come to terms with what just happened," I said, slipping into my wraith wrangler persona.

"Well, that's easy. You did this, Harry. You killed me. You're still holding the bloody knife, for Christ's sakes."

She was right. I let the knife drop from my blood-streaked fingers and it clattered to the floor.

Just then, a voice sounded in the living room. When I recognized it, I looked up with relief bordering on incredulity.

"Harry? Harry, where are you?"

"In here!" I cried.

"Who's that?" asked Mavis. "And how did they get into my flat?"

A stringy young man with flaxen hair and a deep tan came hurrying into the kitchen. When he saw the mess on the floor, he gulped. Jarrett might be my fellow wraith wrangler but that doesn't mean he enjoys the sight of blood.

"Oh my," he said, holding a hand to his face. "This is a disaster!"

"Hey, that's my bloody body lying there dead!" Mavis snapped. "Show some respect. Who are you, anyway? And what are you doing in my flat?"

"This is Jarrett," I said. "Jarrett, meet Mavis, my friend from high school. Jarrett is also a wraith wrangler," I explained to Mavis. "He's my partner."

"Oh, I see. First you kill me then you bring in your assistant to clean up the mess. Is this the moment he starts chucking acid into my bathtub to dissolve my body? Yes, I've seen *Pulp Fiction*. You're Harvey Keitel, aren't you?"

"No, my name is Jarrett Zephyr-Thornton the Third," said Jarrett, simple pride lending his features the nobility his family's vast fortune warranted.

"No, you're the cleaner. You're going to wash me down the drain till there's nothing left! Not a strand of DNA—not a single trace. I'll be erased! Gone!"

"Does your friend always talk this much?" asked Jarrett.

"Yes, I always talk this much," Mavis snapped. "Especially when I've just been murdered by a friend I haven't seen since high school! How was I to know she'd secretly turned into a serial killer with mob connections?!"

Jarrett cut a quick glance at me. "Did you do this, Harry?" Then he held up a smartly gloved hand. "Don't answer that. I don't want to know."

"Of course I didn't do this!" I yelled. "I would never kill anyone, least of all my best friend from school."

"That begs the question: who did?"

I shrugged helplessly. "I don't know! I was passed out in my cake!"

"Oh, is that what that brown stuff on your face is? I thought you'd enjoyed a mud mask." He glanced over at what was left of the cake and took a slice. "Do you mind? I had a very light lunch."

"Don't touch that!" I said. "I passed out after a slice of that cake."

"Isn't it bad enough you killed me?" asked Mavis, clearly offended. "Now you have to go and insult my baking skills?"

"You didn't bake this. You got it from Lidl."

Jarrett uttered a sound of disgust and quickly dropped the cake. Since Lidl wasn't on the list of Royal Warrant holders, it probably was beneath him.

"How did you get here anyway?" I asked Jarrett.

"Buckley told me you were in trouble so I immediately hopped into my Rolls and—ta-dah. Here I am. Your rescuing angel at your service."

"Buckley is here?"

"He's the one who let me into this nice lady's flat."

Mavis narrowed her eyes at Jarrett. "Flattery won't save you, mister. And before you start dissolving my body in some nasty-arse acid, let me tell you—"

Unfortunately her words would be lost to history, as Buckley chose that moment to make his entrance. The frizzy-haired dapper little gentleman zoomed right through the kitchen wall and gave Mavis the fright of her life. Buckley took one look at Mavis and his amiable hobbit face turned grim.

"Nasty business, Harry," he said. "Very nasty business indeed."

"Who are you calling nasty, you Bilbo Baggins wannabe?" Mavis demanded.

"I'm not referring to you, dear lady," said Buckley graciously, "but to the circumstances surrounding your most unfortunate demise."

Mollified, Mavis asked, "And who are you, then?"

"I'm Harry's former employer and now ghost assistant."

"Oh, God. You're here to oversee the body liquefaction, aren't you? You can't do this, sir. I deserve a proper burial same way as the next gal."

Buckley, feeling these were deep waters, blinked once, then turned to me. "You have to get out of here, Harry. You have to leave right this instant."

"But please clean yourself up first," Jarrett suggested. "You're not getting into the Rolls looking like that."

"I can't just leave," I said. "I can't leave Mavis."

"Mavis is dead, Harry," said Buckley. "There's nothing you can do for her. But her blood…" He pointed at the pool at our feet. "… has been dripping through the cracks, alerting the neighbors, who have just called the police."

"Thank God for my neighbors!" Mavis cried. "Bless their Tory-loving hearts!"

"So you see," Buckley continued, "if you don't leave now, you will be arrested for murder." He glanced down at the knife. "As far as I can tell, your prints are all over that knife. And if I'm not mistaken that's the murder weapon."

Mavis had drifted up to Buckley and was studying him closely. "So you're a genuine ghost, eh?"

"Yes, I am," he said with a smile. "And I'm afraid you are, too, my dear."

She heaved a deep sigh. "Yeah, I'm starting to see how that might be true."

Buckley placed his hands on Mavis's ectoplasmic shoulders. "My dear Mavis. Harry didn't do this—I'm positive. I've known Harry for a long time and she's not a murderer. From one ghost to another—trust me on that."

She stared at him. "Of course you would say that. You're Harry's friend, aren't you? So it's only natural for you to try and sow doubts in my mind. But it won't work. Harry did this, Mr. Ghost Man. No one else was here."

"Harry would never do such a thing, Mavis. Never."

"Well, prepare yourself for a big shock. Cause she did. Harry McCabre killed me in cold blood. Yes, she did," she insisted when Buckley started to protest. "She killed me and now she's going to face the consequences."

Chapter Three

We were back at Jarrett's suite at the Ritz-Carlton. Jarrett isn't merely a wraith wrangler, he's also the son of one of the richest men in England, multi-billionaire Jarrett Zephyr-Thornton the Second, after whom he was named. Before becoming a wraith wrangler Jarrett was a jack-of-all trades, but in that very peculiar billionaire set style: he started a space airline, he was on Celebrity Big Brother, dabbled in rock stardom, figure skating, Formula One, Taekwondo... You name it, he did it. Until he found his calling by chasing wraiths and trying to solve their murders with little old me.

"Oh, dear," said Deshawn the minute we stepped into the luxury suite. "You look positively ghastly, Harry. Straight to the bathroom. Chop chop."

I followed him to the bathroom. Deshawn, a stocky man with immaculate manners, is Jarrett's fiancé. He's also Jarrett's former butler, and still enjoys running the household at Casa Zephyr. He now led me to the marble-floor bathroom with the gold fixtures and instructed me to strip off my bloodied clothes, place them on the floor, and give myself a good long scrub.

But not before enveloping me in a hug.

"Oh, Harry," he said. "I'm so sorry about what happened to your friend."

I stifled a sob. "It's horrible, Deshawn. It's all so terribly horrible."

"I know, darling," he said, holding me at arm's length for a moment while fixing me with an encouraging smile. "But

EXCERPT FROM GHOSTLIER THINGS (GHOSTS OF LONDO...

we're going to get to the bottom of this, I promise you. Now go and stand under that shower for half an hour, and don't come out until you're squeaky clean. And don't worry about your clothes. I'll simply throw them into the incinerator and have a fresh set laid out for you when you're done."

"The incinerator? You're going to burn my clothes?"

"Of course I am. We can't have you involved in this nasty crime, can we? Did you remove your fingerprints from the murder weapon?"

"Yes, I did," I said, flashing back to the moment Jarrett had taken the knife between thumb and forefinger and dropped it into the dishwasher along with the cups and saucers and forks and knives Mavis and I had used. In spite of Mavis's protestations Jarrett had quickly pushed the button and had then proceeded to wipe every possible surface to remove any other trace of me.

"But it's not right, Deshawn," I said now. "I shouldn't be doing this."

"You should if you don't want to go to prison for murder," he insisted.

"But if I didn't do it, who did?"

"We'll figure it out," he promised. "Now shoo. Get yourself cleaned up." He glanced down at my fingers. "Is that blood? Please scrape scrape scrape."

"Oh, God. I'm a killer, aren't I?"

"No you're not, darling. The Harry McCabre I know and love wouldn't hurt a fly. Whoever did this is trying to frame you."

And with these words, and after giving me another warm smile, he left the bathroom.

I stood under that shower for what felt like hours. As the spray nozzles pummeled me from all sides, and the dinner-plate-sized shower head pounded down on me from above, I slowly started to feel human again.

I soaped myself up at least three times, and rinsed off the delicious-smelling—and probably extremely expensive—shower gel with a purple loofah each time, to get the grime and horror of the murder out of my system and my body. When I finally finished, I walked out of the shower cabin into a steamed-up bathroom, a set of fresh clothes placed on the pink marble sink like Deshawn had promised.

I slipped into the Saint Laurent skinny jeans and Chanel T-shirt and found them to be exactly my size. In spite of the circumstances I produced a feeble smile. Deshawn was amazing. He'd even gotten me a pair of Raf Simons sneakers, and, like the clothes, they were a perfect fit, my feet slipping into them as if they were tailor-made.

I walked out of the bathroom and found my friends in conference in the spacious and perfectly-appointed kitchen. Jarrett, Sir Buckley and Deshawn all looked up when I walked in, their faces etched with expressions of concern.

"Oh, Harry," said Jarrett the moment I stepped into the kitchen. "How are you holding up, darling?"

"I'm fine," I assured him. "It's not me you should be worrying about. It's Mavis. We have to find out who did this to her."

"Whoever it was, they're obviously trying to set you up," said Jarrett. "And there's no way I'm going to let you go to jail for a crime you didn't commit."

"You weren't there by any chance, were you Buckley?" I asked the aged ghost, who was directing a longing look at the tiny shrimp salad sandwiches placed on a silver platter on the counter.

"No, I wasn't, I'm afraid," he said. "I was down at the Hippodrome when I had a sudden premonition something terrible was happening with you. So I immediately rushed across town and arrived just in time to see you passed out on the kitchen floor, a knife in your hand, and your friend dead next to you."

"Wait, I was passed out on the floor, right?" I asked as memory returned.

"Yes, you were, clutching the big bloody butcher knife in your hand."

"But when I passed out I wasn't anywhere near the floor. I was on the balcony. I'd taken a sip of my tea when the world suddenly turned dark."

"So whoever killed Mavis must have drugged either your tea or your cake, and then moved you so it would look like you killed her," said Jarrett thoughtfully.

"Well, at least we managed to thwart their devious plan," said Buckley. "No way the police will be able to connect you to the crime now."

"But we still have to solve Mavis's murder," I said. "That's our priority."

"Our priority is to keep you as far away from this case as possible," said Deshawn. "You can't be seen anywhere near Mavis or her flat, Harry."

"Did anyone see you enter the building?" asked Jarrett.

"Maybe—I don't know. I didn't really pay attention."

Suddenly the bell to the flat chimed and we all looked up.

"Are we expecting someone, Deshawn?" asked Jarrett.

"No, sir," said Deshawn, swiftly slipping into his butler routine, as was his habit when the doorbell rang. Like a horse pricking up its ears at the sound of the racing bell, Deshawn's butlering had a habit of resurfacing at odd times.

He moved to the door with professional alacrity, head held high, posture rigid, expression supercilious. I heard him answer the door and I shared a look of concern with Jarrett. Moments later, Darian Watley came walking into the kitchen, followed by a heavyset woman with flaming red hair and an apologetic look on her face, Deshawn, still in full butler mode, trailing them.

"Inspector Darian Watley of the Metropolitan Police Service," Deshawn announced from the door with perfect diction, "accompanied by Inspector Tilda Fret, also employed by Scotland Yard. Here on official police business."

"Darian? What are you doing here?" I asked.

Darian, a large and handsome man who could have been a professional swimsuit model if he hadn't opted for a career in law enforcement—and also my boyfriend—gave me a look of concern. "Harry? I'm afraid I have to take you in for questioning in connection with the murder of Mavis Bletchley."

ABOUT NIC

Nic has a background in political science and before being struck by the writing bug worked odd jobs around the world (including but not limited to massage therapist in Mexico, gardener in Italy, restaurant manager in India, and Berlitz teacher in Belgium).

When he's not writing he enjoys curling up with a good (comic) book, watching British crime dramas, French comedies or Nancy Meyers movies, sampling pastry (apple cake!), pasta and chocolate (preferably the dark variety), twisting himself into a pretzel doing morning yoga, going for a brisk walk, and spoiling his feline assistants Lily and Ricky.

He lives with his wife (and aforementioned cats) in a small village smack dab in the middle of absolutely nowhere and is probably writing his next book right now.

www.nicsaint.com

Printed in Great Britain
by Amazon